BETTER NOT BET A BLUESTOCKING

Ladies of Opportunity
Book Three

By
Collette Cameron®

Blue Rose Romance® *LLC*

Sweet-to-Spicy Timeless Romance®

storage and retrieval system, without the written permission of the publisher, except where permitted by law.

For permission requests, contact the publisher at the email below.

collette@collettecameronbooks.com

collettecameronbooks.com

eBook ISBN: 978-1-966087-52-6
Print Book ISBN: 978-1-966087-53-3

. . .

FREE BOOK!

JOIN MY EXCLUSIVE MAILING LIST
Collette Cameron Newsletter

AND GET A FREE EBOOK!

https://collettecameronbooks.com/freegift

Plus Sneak Peeks, Giveaways, Contests, Exclusive Content, and More... P.S. I promise only good stuff ~ **no** spam!

DEDICATION

For W., my treasured first grandson—
Even before I hold you in my arms,
you've already filled a space in my heart.
You are deeply loved, always and forever.
Gigi

PRAISE FOR...

BETTER NOT BET A BLUESTOCKING

See What Readers Are Saying About
Better Not Bet a Bluestocking!

See What Readers Are Saying About
Better Not Bet a Bluestocking!

★★★★★ "The witty conversations between them, Georgina's little sister, who is a flirt, and an old gossip who tries to create a scandal, make the story interesting and humorous." ~ *Marilyn*

★★★★★ "A charming novella that proves love doesn't need scandal to sizzle, and this one delivers a gentle romance with emotional depth, quick pacing, and a couple whose mutual devotion and guarded hearts feel refreshingly real." ~ *Lana Birky*

★★★★★ "The witty conversations between them,

Georgina's little sister, who is a flirt, and an old gossip who tries to create a scandal, make the story interesting and humorous. This is a cute, short, sweet romance." ~ *Hooviecat*

★★★★★ " This story was enjoyable, and the time flew by while I was reading. I adore Robyn, he was so nice and easy going.' ~ *Rosemary Muldoon*

ONE

Outskirts of London
Fernleigh House Garden

Early May 1819—late afternoon

Are we going to die?

Rigid and trembling, Georgine Thackerly stood beside her closest friends—Roxina Danforth, Matilda Fitzlloyd, Aubriella Matherfield, and Claire Granlund in the Fitzlloyds' magnificent garden.

Rufus Desmond—dangerous and despicable with a soul blacker than the Earl of Hell's waistcoat—had dared to trespass into the private sanctuary and now stood with a gloating grin spreading across his face. According to Roxina, the blackguard would just as easily shoot them as stomp upon a beetle with his boot heel.

Icy dread engulfed Georgine.

"You are trespassing, sir." Matilda swallowed before

continuing, her voice tremulous but even. "I must ask you to leave at once before I send for the constable."

"Not without Miss Danforth," Desmond responded with arrogant confidence.

"As there are five of us and only three of you, how do you propose to take Roxina?" Aubriella challenged him, and Georgine couldn't help but admire her bravado.

He waved his pistol, sunlight gleaming off the barrel, as his two unsavory compatriots openly ogled the women. His voice steeped in smugness, Desmond said, "We are armed, and I seriously doubt you ladies have a pistol or a knife hidden in your skirts."

Something Georgine would seriously consider in the future. That and shooting lessons.

If she survived this ordeal.

She raised her chin in challenge. "Yes, but we can scream and cause a ruckus. People will come running."

She sounded far more confident than she felt.

"That would be foolish." Shaking his head, Desmond let out a dramatic sigh. "I'll shoot the first woman who screams."

The women gasped in unison.

Georgine had no doubt the fiend would shoot them, without compunction or remorse.

Desmond shifted his pistol toward Roxina. "I still intend to take Miss Danforth, with or without your cooperation."

"If I come willingly," Roxina said evenly, "will you leave my friends unharmed?"

"No, Roxina," Georgine whispered.

Desmond tilted his head in mock consideration.

"There's no need for you to sacrifice yourself, Roxina." Shelby Tellinger eased through the opening in the gate behind Desmond.

Caught by surprise, Desmond stiffened.

The madman's carelessness sent a tiny quiver of hope skipping along Georgine's pulse.

An instant later, Robyn Fitzlloyd slipped into view.

Both men wielded guns.

Her pulse jumped again, and relief coursed through her. All hope was not lost. Never had Georgine been so glad to see Robyn...and Shelby too, of course.

Surely Desmond would leave now.

What choice did he have?

"I would not move, not even to breathe." Pistol drawn, Robyn stepped forward. His usual affable air had hardened into something cold and menacing.

Georgine shivered, never having seen this ferocious side of him before.

He swept a glance over the women—pausing on his sister, then Georgine for half a second—before leveling his gun at Desmond's henchmen. "I'll thank you to stop pointing your weapons at the women."

"You and Tellinger have but a single shot." Desmond waved his pistol between himself and his men. "You cannot shoot all three of us."

"But there are three of us, as well."

Startled, Desmond turned as Quentin Honeybrook stepped out from behind a laurel bush, his weapon raised and his stare murderous. "And I'll wager this commotion has servants and townspeople descending upon the gardens within seconds. This is a battle you shall not win."

"Oh, thank God," Claire whispered beside Georgine. "We are saved."

Not yet; we aren't.

"Ladies, move toward the house. Slowly," Honeybrook instructed, his tone flat and icy.

"The first one that takes a step gets a lead ball," Desmond's taller companion countered before spitting on the ground.

"Hold your tongue, Carver." Desmond speared the man a murderous glare. "*I* give the orders."

Then, the callous beast raised his pistol and aimed the barrel straight at Roxina.

Georgine's blood congealed in her veins, and her lungs constricted so she couldn't suck in any air.

A growling, furry canine blur hurtled into the scene—Dash, Roxina's faithful hound.

Desmond staggered as Dash collided with him.

A gunshot cracked like thunder, sending a bird to flight.

A woman screamed, but Georgine didn't know who.

Two more shots rang out in quick succession.

The scarred man beside Desmond collapsed with a neat hole in his forehead. His pistol clattered beside him.

Oh, my God.

Bile billowed up Georgine's throat. She'd never seen anyone shot before. Waves of nausea slammed into her, and faintness caused a myriad of tiny black dots to dance before her eyes.

Desmond roared as Dash sank his teeth into the man's arm. With his free hand, Desmond yanked a blade free from beneath his coat.

"Dash!" Roxina cried in terror for her beloved pet.

"Stay back, Roxina!" Tellinger lunged forward.

Desmond lifted his blade to strike the snarling animal.

Honeybrook didn't hesitate. With one eye closed, he aimed and discharged his gun.

Desmond's head snapped back, and before Georgine could blink, he hit the ground. The knife slid from his hand, blood pooling beneath his skull.

Oh, my God. Oh, my God. Oh, my God.

Searing heat bloomed in Georgine's shoulder. She glanced downward, even as she touched the crimson staining her gown. Blood coated her fingertips.

Blood?

She blinked in confusion.

"Georgine?" Matilda's alarmed voice, faint and muffled, seemed to come through a long tunnel.

"Oh, my God." Aubriella flung an arm around Georgine. "You've been shot, Georgie."

"I don't feel any pain." Georgine blinked, trying to focus her fuzzy vision. "So why am I bleeding?"

"She's in shock." Claire's voice trembled. "Someone should notify her sister."

Everything became hazy, making it hard to see and hear.

A second later, Robyn lifted Georgine into his arms. He spoke to her, but she couldn't quite catch his words.

Was that tenderness in his hooded brown eyes?

Robyn *never* regarded her tenderly.

Mocking, derisive, exasperated, superior, and sardonic?

Indeed, and often.

The blood loss must be causing her to imagine things.

"Robyn Fitzlloyd, put me down," she demanded, rather weakly. "What will people say?"

"If I put you down, you'll collapse." Jaw clenched, he marched toward the house. "Besides, I'd sooner tend a flea's hiccup than fret about gossip."

"Bossy brute."

Then, the world slipped away.

TWO

Still on the Fernleigh House grounds

An indeterminable number of agonizing seconds later

Robyn tried to keep from bouncing Georgine too much as he raced toward the house, shouting orders.

"Someone, go for the doctor.

"Also, the constable.

"We need hot water and linens for bandages.

"What are you waiting for?"

Servants scrambled to do his bidding.

He glanced over his shoulder, never breaking his rapid pace.

"Matilda, which chamber?"

His sister flew to his side. "The rose bedchamber, I think."

Yes, a good choice.

It had the most natural light—better for the physician to remove the ball.

Robyn's gut clenched merely thinking about the dangerous and painful procedure.

As he charged across the garden path, he fought clawing panic and another unnamed, but powerful emotion that crushed his ribs in a vice-like grip and tightened his throat to the point of choking.

He dropped his attention to the feminine bundle clenched in his arms as he raced into the house.

There's so much blood.

Sweet Georgine's blood.

Ashen, her mouth slightly parted, and her sable eyelashes fanning her white cheeks, for an instant, he thought she had died in his arms.

No, God, no.

Georgine cannot die.

She cannot.

Then her chest rose in a shallow breath, and such blessed relief thrummed through him that hot moisture stung his eyes.

Thank God.

Matilda flew up the stairs ahead of him and, boots pounding, Robyn bolted after his sister.

Once inside the pretty but dated bedchamber, Matilda yanked the coverlet back before flying to open the floral draperies. The drapes and bedcovers, in mellowed shades of crimson and green upon an ivory background, retained their richness despite three decades of careful use, their pattern a little old-fashioned but still genteel.

His heart aching, Robyn tenderly laid Georgine upon the rosewood four-poster bed.

Moaning softly, she moved her head back and forth, as if trying to escape the torturous pain.

"Here, Robyn." Matilda unceremoniously thrust a towel she had snatched from the nightstand at him. "To staunch the bleeding."

Robyn swiftly folded the linen and pressed it to the oozing wound.

She must stop bleeding.

"I'll fetch a nightgown." She dashed out of the chamber before he could respond.

Where was the bloody doctor?

The servants with the bandages and hot water?

Georgine moaned again.

Her pain nearly eviscerated him.

Stupid fool.

He had disregarded his growing feelings toward her for years, firmly believing she wouldn't be receptive to his fond esteem. That was all he allowed himself to call his affection, for acknowledging the sentiment was something more, made him vulnerable.

Besides, he rather enjoyed their verbal sparring and matching wits with her. She possessed a keen intellect and an uncommon strategic logic. But now that she lay bleeding, possibly fighting for her life, he could only castigate himself for being a coward and an idiot.

Dolt.

Bufflehead.

Lackbrain.

"You cannot die, Georgine. I shan't let you."

Bending nearer, Robyn dared to press his lips to her clammy forehead. Not a romantic first kiss, for certain.

His voice, a harsh rasp, he choked, "I cannot imagine a world without you in it."

Never had truer words been uttered.

A moment later, his sister, carrying a nightgown and chemise, a maid bearing a stack of linens—no doubt to use as bandages, a footman lugging two buckets of hot water, and Doctor Thaddeus Tinsdale clasping his black leather physician's bag, piled into the bedchamber.

At once, the doctor expertly assessed the situation and took immediate control. Without preamble or an apology, he shoved Robyn aside to examine Georgine's wound. "Everyone out. Except Miss Fitzlloyd. You can help me undress the patient."

"Her name is Georgine Thackerly." Robyn took a few reluctant steps backward.

Never had he felt so utterly helpless or inadequate.

The doctor sent him a hard sideways look. "Make yourself useful. Go to the kitchen and have the cook prepare bone broth and yarrow root tea. And we'll need more hot water." He looked beneath the blood-soaked towel. "A lot more."

Robyn nodded.

"Is she...?" Unable to tear his gaze from Georgine, he cleared his throat. "Is she going to be all right, Doctor?"

Matilda raised her head and, her clear blue eyes narrowed, gave him a speculative glance, as if she had suddenly guessed his secret.

"This is a very grave injury, Mr. Fitzlloyd." Without looking in Robyn's direction again, the doctor muttered, "I hope to save her arm, but in truth, only time will tell."

Robyn scarcely remembered leaving the bedchamber and making his way to the kitchen to speak to Mrs. Fennick and convey the physician's orders. Afterward, he wandered into his study. He plopped onto a leather wingback chair and stared morosely at the unlit fireplace.

Resting his head against the chair's back, he peered at the ceiling.

Georgine lay up there, suffering only God knew what.

He firmed his mouth in resolution.

If Georgine recovered—no, *when* she was well—he meant to explore these conflicting feelings for the spirited bluestocking.

Even if the outcome wasn't to his liking.

THREE

Fernleigh House
Rose bedchamber

May 1819—evening

Georgine swallowed a moan.

She wasn't dead then.

Dead people didn't feel pain. So great was the agony thrumming in her shoulder that, for an instant, she wished she *had* expired.

Sweet Jesus, has someone impaled me with a molten fireplace poker?

Memories came flooding back.

Not stabbed—shot.

Sharp, throbbing heat radiated from the wound, and each breath sent a fresh, tormenting lance through her. An insidious, clawing pain dug into her flesh and refused to relent. Her feeble attempt to shift only worsened her discomfort, and a small, ragged gasp escaped her lips before she could suppress it.

Eyes closed, she struggled to recall the details of the shooting.

That blackguard Desmond and his thugs stormed into the garden, threatening Roxina and the others. Then Shelby Tellinger appeared—Robyn Fitzlloyd and Quentin Honeybrook too.

Georgine scrunched her eyebrows together, relieved when the minuscule movement did not cause another stab of agony.

Then what?

Oh, yes.

She remembered now.

Several volleys of gunfire had been exchanged, killing Desmond and one of his men.

Georgine vaguely recalled Aubriella exclaiming, "You've been shot, Georgie."

How peculiar that I didn't feel any pain in the garden, yet now this burning in my shoulder makes me nauseous and nearly causes me to swoon.

A tremor of consternation rippled through Georgine, making her break out in an icy sweat.

She had been shot.

Not merely grazed, but wounded severely enough to render her insensible. She remembered objecting to Robyn scooping her into his arms and racing toward the house, shouting orders, but nothing after that.

What if the bullet had shattered bone?

Had she lost the use of her arm?

What if an infection sets in?

Muted whispering roused Georgine further, but she didn't have the strength to open her eyes at the moment.

"How is she?" a man asked, his tone low.

Robyn Fitzlloyd—

Not quite Georgine's nemesis, though a constant, irksome pebble in her slipper, he now spoke with a note of concern that seemed almost genuine—a disconcerting novelty from his lips.

"Doctor Tinsdale believes Georgie will probably not rouse until morning, Robyn," his sister, Matilda, said. "She lost a significant amount of blood, and the shock alone is enough to keep her abed for some time. He's wrapped her arm against her torso to prevent any movement of her shoulder."

Doctor Tinsdale?

A doctor has been here?

What was Georgine's prognosis?

"Did he leave instructions?" Robyn asked, a touch of impatience tempering the question.

Because of the inconvenience Georgine had caused his household?

She could hardly be faulted for taking a lead ball meant for another.

How long had she been unconscious, anyway?

"The physician removed the ball and sterilized and bandaged the wound, but because the bone was chipped, Doctor Tinsdale would like her monitored throughout the night." Utter exhaustion leached into Matilda's voice. "He left laudanum. Georgine will be in extreme pain when she awakens. He also advised that movement will worsen her discomfort, so we are to keep her as still as possible. Oh, and only small sips of water tonight. She'll be thirsty, but he does not want to risk her vomiting and tearing the sutures."

"Understandable," Robyn murmured.

The sound of paper crackling carried to Georgine.

"He left a daily regimen, too, and said he would leave instructions with Mrs. Fennick on how to prepare the various tonics as well as what Georgine should eat to help her heal." The paper rustled again. "She is to have warm bone broth with a spoonful of honey and garlic syrup in the morning. Midday, yarrow or thyme tea. Evening: elderberry cordial or chamomile tea with honey, and as needed, garlic-vinegar-honey tonic, but only small sips."

None of which sounded the least appealing.

In truth, revolting better described Georgine's invalid's menu.

Robyn made a rough sound in his throat.

Annoyance? Displeasure? Frustration?

Disgust at the unappetizing menu?

"I'm relieved that's not my fare. Poor Georgine." Again, a note of genuine concern tempered his reply.

Well, that answered that question.

Georgine released a long, shallow breath.

How much would a chipped bone delay her recovery, and what did that mean for the use of her arm?

Alarm thrummed through her.

Would she have the use of her arm?

Matilda murmured something Georgine could not make out.

"Ah, I see." Robyn's tone was impossible to decipher. "Well, this should prove quite interesting."

What should?

"Doctor Tinsdale will call in the morning to check on her progress," Matilda said, scarcely above an exhausted whisper.

"You look done in, Mittie." Weariness and affection tempered Robyn's mellow baritone. "Why don't you take a dinner tray in your room and then retire for the night? It is nearly half of nine already. Since it's unlikely Miss Thackerly will awaken, I'll have Agnes sit with her."

Robyn might be a controlling bugger, but he adored his younger sister.

"Oh, Robyn." Genuine dismay colored Matilda's exclamation. "With all the commotion, I forgot to tell you. Agnes's mother took a nasty fall this afternoon." Fabric rustled a few feet away. "She will be absent for several days."

A resigned masculine sigh echoed throughout the chamber.

"I shall stay with Georgine then." He did not sound thrilled at the prospect. "You need to rest."

Wait.

Hold on a moment.

Georgine's sluggish mind tripped over itself.

Robyn will what?

He cannot stay here.

With me.

Alone.

"Are you sure, Robyn? You must check her wound for bleeding, oozing, and signs of infection every two hours." Concern and a touch of doubt edged Matilda's question. "Besides, it is highly improper for you to be with Georgine unchaperoned. You know how fussy she is about propriety. If she were to awaken, she would object most strenuously."

Yes, I most certainly would!

I do!

I object most vehemently!

Why couldn't Georgine speak?

Even as her mind raced, her tongue seemed swollen to twice its normal size, and the ability to form words proved beyond her.

"Well, given she's as white as the sheets she is lying upon and in a near stupor to boot, she cannot object, can she?" Warm and unrepentant humor riddled Robyn's tone. "What she doesn't know cannot hurt her. Besides, her reputation is the least of her worries right now."

The least...?

The gall of the cocky bounder!

If Georgine could crack her eyes open, she would incinerate him with a murderous glare.

However, the simple movement would require more effort than she could summon, and besides, the infernal man probably smirked like a gargoyle, which would only annoy her further. She could hear the jollity in his voice—the smug certainty, the mischievous lilt that suggested he was wholly unbothered by decorum or propriety.

The arrogance!

The sheer audacity!

This is not a minor infraction—this is...ruinous.

The moment someone discovers that he remained alone with me overnight, my reputation will be in tatters.

There will be whispers.

Speculation.

Perhaps even demands that he do the honorable thing and— good God—marry me.

FOUR

Still in her bedchamber at Fernleigh House

Several unimaginably frantic heartbeats later

NO!

No, no, no.

I cannot bear the thought of being shackled to any man, but most especially that insufferable, controlling—

Horror slowly unfurled in Georgine's chest.

Her shoulder throbbed anew, a cruel reminder of her delicate condition.

Robyn *must* leave.

Not normally given to flying into a dither or entertaining nonsensical imaginations, she blamed her wound and the persistent pain on her elevated emotional state.

The bed shifted a fraction, as though he had moved nearer and bumped the mattress as he loomed above her.

A touch so light she might have fabricated it.

"I imagine the pain is nearly unbearable," he said beneath his breath. "I would wager a swallow of brandy would not go amiss either."

For him or her?

She would take more than a swallow, thank you very much. An unladylike gulp, or better yet, half a bottle. No, an *entire* bottle.

Not that she regularly indulged in strong spirits.

In truth, she had only ever tasted brandy once...

She had been fourteen, and her father had passed out in another drunken stupor, only this time, a few drops of brandy remained in his glass.

A rarity indeed, given his penchant for the spirit.

Curious to learn what about the strong spirit caused him to become an angry, violent monster, she had dared to taste the umber liquid. The brandy had burned hot and sharp upon her tongue, its bitter bite singeing her throat and leaving behind a cloying heaviness that made her cough.

Georgine had not liked the taste and had no desire to sample it again, but such was her pain at the moment, she would down a glass, coughing and sputtering, if the unpleasant liquor provided her with any relief.

She caught a whisper of movement, the faintest rasp of fabric, and then, impossibly gently, Robyn ghosted a calloused fingertip over the uninjured part of her arm, also wrapped to prevent movement.

Upon my word.

A goose trussed for Michaelmas supper could move more than she.

It took Georgine a moment to realize Robyn merely checked her injury.

Regardless, her breath caught, but she forced herself to remain still, to feign unconsciousness. She could not let him know she was awake—not when her mind swirled with indignation, not when outrage burned hotter than the pain in her shoulder.

Georgine prided herself on her ability to display decorum, even when not at her best. But as assuredly as she had been wounded, such control was beyond her at this moment.

Robyn cannot stay.

He absolutely cannot stay.

Suffocating and relentless, the night closed in, helplessness wrapping around Georgine like a shroud.

How dare he decide this for me?

How dare he assume I would accept such impropriety?

Jaw clenched, she twitched her fingers against the sheet.

Georgine tried to open her eyes and speak, but her mouth felt as dry as cold fireplace ash. No matter how she willed her lids to lift, they remained heavy, weighted by exhaustion and pain.

I am as helpless as a day-old lamb.

Frustration burned behind her breastbone.

For two years after her mother passed on to her eternal reward, Georgine had managed the household. Since her father's passing ten years ago, no man had dictated her choices. She had decided for herself and her sister since she was sixteen, and done well too, thank you very much.

God above, she resented the sudden presumption that a man, least of all Robyn, had the right to speak for her now.

She had fought for every ounce of independence, ensuring her younger sister never lacked food, shelter, protection, or the right to voice her opinion. Not a simple task in a world dominated and governed by men.

Now, after mere hours in Robyn Fitzlloyd's house, he had taken control of everything: her recovery, her choices, even her ability to move.

Trapped.

Dependent.

At the mercy of another's will.

The very reasons she had never considered marriage.

She'd witnessed what her father's absolute control and unrelenting imposition of his will had done to her mother.

No one ever breathed the words aloud, but Mama had never been happier than after Father died.

A different sort of panic washed over Georgine.

Material swished nearby again.

Matilda murmured something, then the door latch clicked.

She had left—left Georgine alone with Robyn Fitzlloyd.

Georgine could not be angry with her friend, but neither could she accept this situation.

A chair creaked, followed by a hefty sigh—Robyn settling in as though he intended to stay for the duration.

Heat simmered beneath Georgine's breastbone.

Absolutely not.

She parted her lips and tried to tell him just that, but only a dry rasp escaped.

"Are you awake, Miss Thackerly?" Boots scuffed against the wooden floorboards, and the air shifted as his presence loomed closer again. "How is your pain?"

Godawful, you daft man.

But her thirst was worse.

"Thir...thirst..." She swallowed against the dryness, muting her. "Thirs-ty."

Glass clinked against the nightstand, followed by the gentle pour of water cascading from a decanter, and then another soft clank she could not identify.

"I'll have to raise you a couple of inches, Miss Thackerly, else you could choke."

The mattress dipped as Robyn leaned in.

He slipped a firm arm beneath her back and lifted her carefully, supporting her weight with a strength that unsettled her.

Fire streaked through her shoulder, sharp and relentless.

Her eyes flew open, and she tightened her fingers on the counterpane, forcing back an agonized gasp.

"Easy," Robyn murmured, his voice low and steady. "I have you."

The scent of grass, musk, and gunpowder clung to him, as did a faint trace of sandalwood. A distracting combination—earthy and dangerously enticing.

And something she had absolutely no business noticing.

He touched the glass's cool rim to her lips, then tilted it slightly, allowing a few drops of sweet water to trickle onto her parched tongue.

Blessed relief.

The ache in her throat eased, but her thirst still demanded more.

She had heard that losing a great deal of blood made a person thirsty.

Georgine swallowed greedily, angling forward for another sip of the slightly odd tasting water.

Robyn cruelly pulled the glass away before she could drink more.

"I think that is enough for now," he said. "I'll give you more in a few minutes, but I do not want you taking in too much too soon. It could make you nauseous."

Frustration rippled through Georgine.

She wanted more.

She gazed longingly at the glass, itching to seize it and drain every drop.

"I am *not* a child." She scowled, leveling him with a blistering glare.

His lips twitched before he brought them under control and arranged his features into a benign expression. "No, indeed."

Insufferable man.

The glass met the nightstand with a soft clink before he lowered her back onto the pillows, adjusting them with careful, if slightly clumsy, hands.

With a slight flutter, she raised her eyelids.

Robyn Fitzlloyd loomed close, too close.

Golden candlelight carved sharp shadows along his firm, beard-stubbled jaw, the proud arch of his hawkish brows, and the sharp focus in his deep brown eyes. Dark blond hair tumbled over his forehead in unruly waves, evidence of his habit of raking his fingers through it.

Grass stains marred his waistcoat, and a streak of dirt smudged his sleeve.

He had risked his life today too.

Fighting to keep her eyelids open, she swallowed against the lingering dryness in her throat. "You haven't changed your attire since the garden debacle?"

"And leave you to awaken unattended?" He quirked an eyebrow, his usual humor back in place. "You wound me, Miss Thackerly. I thought we were friends."

"*Friends*?" She pointed an arch gaze at him. "That *is* quite a stretch."

His mouth twitched again, amusement lingering at the corners.

He had a nice mouth.

She must be delirious, noticing a man's mouth.

"I am..." She swallowed hard. "I am sorry."

His expression grew puzzled. "I fail to see what you have to be sorry for."

"I'm sorry to be an inconvenience." She pressed her hands

against the soft counterpane, curling her fingers slightly. "I shall return home in the morning, and your household can return to normal."

She loathed how frail she sounded. But then again, she had a valid reason.

A deep chuckle rumbled from his chest.

Irritation pricked Georgine.

Did he think this situation called for humor?

Pain gnawed at her shoulder, depleting her usual good nature and patience.

Her sister waited at home, alone, and yet *this man*—this insufferable, laughing rogue—found something amusing in Georgine's plight.

"I fail to see what is so humorous, Mr. Fitzlloyd." She aimed for firmness, but the words emerged breathy and weak.

His nut-brown eyes gleamed.

"Forgive me, Miss Thackerly, but the physician gave strict orders that you are not to rise from this bed for *at least* a fortnight. The ball has been surgically removed, but you've suffered a chipped bone. I doubt he'll agree to let you travel for at least a month. In truth, probably longer."

A month?

Longer?

Her stomach dropped, as did her jaw.

That could not be right.

"That is impossible." Georgine might have stomped her foot in frustration if she had been standing. Instead, she pursed her lips—not nearly as satisfying.

"Quite the rub, I agree, but there is no help for it." Robyn clasped the back of his neck, his expression unreadable. "I shall not defy the physician's directives."

She blinked groggily.

Good Lord, she could barely stay awake.

Still, concern for her sister compelled her to grit her teeth and tighten her jaw against the seductive slumber beckoning.

"What of my sister, Robyn? Regina sprained her ankle yesterday and cannot bear weight upon it for at least a week." Why did her speech sound slurred? "She is alone. How will she manage? Does she even know what has happened to me?"

He gave a grave nod. "Claire Granlund volunteered to inform your sister and to stay with her as long as necessary."

Claire was a dear friend.

"Your friends send their love." He shrugged and gave her an apologetic glance. "The doctor will not allow them to visit for some time, but he said your sister could."

A bit—but only a tiny bit—of Georgine's worry abated. "Regina will fret. It's her nature to worry."

"You may send a correspondence to her daily," Robyn said smoothly, as if soothing an overwrought child. "Matilda can write it for you. Once Regina is fit to travel, she can come here to stay for the duration of your recovery."

Annoyingly logical.

Georgine loathed being indebted to anyone.

But drat it all—he had thought of everything.

Her sister would be safe and cared for.

"Did the surgeon say how long my recuperation might take?" The question took almost her last ounce of energy.

He ran a hand through his hair. "If all goes well and no infection sets in, at least several weeks."

A long silence stretched between Georgine and Robyn.

Finally, she exhaled, grudging but reconciled to the inevitable. She would do her part to mend quickly and finish her convalescence in her own bed at the earliest opportunity. "I know my presence is an imposition. Thank you."

Robyn let out a slow breath, his mouth tilting into a satisfied half-smile.

"There now. Was that so difficult, my fiery bluestocking?"

A spark of irritation flared to life.

Georgine Emily-Jane Edwina Thackerly, you absolute half-wit!

Why had she yielded to good manners and thanked him—given him even a hint of satisfaction?

This man—this grinning, self-satisfied scoundrel—had seized control of her fate, and instead of issuing a scathing retort, she had *thanked* the vexing man?

And there was the other matter that had her in a pelter of nerves—her reputation.

"Please keep my presence here as discreet as possible, Robyn."

Lord, Georgine could barely keep her eyes open.

"My repute depends on it, as does Regina's. You might not fret about gossip, but you are not an unmarried woman with a sister dependent on her. Flapping tongues fanning the flames of hearsay and conjecture could destroy us both."

His features folding into a serious expression, Robyn nodded. "I understand and assure you, the household will do everything we can to protect your good standing."

For the first time, the umber-colored bottle on the nightstand caught her attention. "You put laudanum in my water."

It wasn't a question.

"Aye," Robyn admitted without a jot of compunction. "You'll heal faster if your pain is kept under control and if you sleep."

Her exhausted body betrayed her yet again, dragging her under before she could give him a piece of her mind.

And she was not *his* fiery bluestocking.

"Rest, Georgine." As the darkness crept over her, Robyn's tone softened to almost tenderness, and he pulled the counterpane up. "I truly regret that you were injured. I promise, I shall take good care of you."

A flicker of warmth curled uninvited in her chest.

Then, just as she teetered on the edge of sleep, he added in a sarcastic drawl, "I hope you don't completely disrupt my household overly much."

Her last conscious thought formed, unwavering and resolute.

Oh, Robyn Fitzlloyd, you can bet this fiery bluestocking shall do her best to do just that!

FIVE

Outside Georgine's chamber at Fernleigh House

Six days later—half of eleven in the evening

Head lowered, one hand cupping his nape while resting a hip against the windowsill, Robyn waited for Doctor Tinsdale to finish examining Georgine. The lone candle in the brass wall sconce flickered, as if objecting to remaining lit this late.

When Robyn had stopped in to check on Georgine before retiring, as he had every night since she'd become his forced guest, her pale, clammy skin and flushed cheeks had immediately alarmed him.

Instead of sleeping, as he had expected, Georgine lay awake, her eyes glassy and lines of pain bracketing her dry lips. She held herself unnaturally still and winced whenever she moved the slightest.

When he touched the back of his hand to her forehead and was met with searing heat, Robyn promptly sent a footman to rouse Doctor Tinsdale from his comfortable bed, despite the lateness of the hour.

However, Robyn hadn't awakened Matilda.

The brunt of Georgine's care had fallen to her, and she needed to sleep.

Besides, what could she have done?

Only this morning, while breaking their fast, he and Matilda had discussed how fortunate Georgine was to have avoided an infection in her wound. Her sister was supposed to arrive tomorrow and remain until Georgine had fully recovered.

Matilda didn't say as much, but she looked forward to more feminine company.

Robyn, on the other hand, very much anticipated his household returning to its normal cadence. More on point, he welcomed not having a very beautiful invalid a few doors down from his bedchamber and disrupting his sleep.

The past week had been pandemonium.

First, Roxina and Shelby had descended upon the house in the middle of the night, chased by that madman Desmond, God rot his black soul. Now, Georgine recovered from a serious wound, and though sweet and polite, Regina Thackerly was a bit of a self-centered scatterbrain—the exact opposite of her poised, considerate, bluestocking older sister.

How could kin be so different?

Lifting his gaze from the floor, Robyn stared at the closed bedchamber door. A frown drew his eyebrows together and his mouth downward.

The longer Doctor Tinsdale remained closeted inside, the more troubled Robyn became.

It seemed his and Matilda's celebration about Georgine's good health had been premature. He hadn't let himself contemplate anything other than her complete recovery, though he knew full well that a chipped bone likely meant some reduced mobility in the shoulder and arm.

Doctor Tinsdale had forbidden mention of that possibility to Georgine, however. He insisted such unwelcome news might affect her mending. Her well-being—physical and mental—was the physician's paramount concern.

Pulling on an earlobe, Robyn contemplated his feelings toward Georgine.

In short, they baffled him.

Last week, during those first few hours, when her life hung in the balance, he would have sworn he loved her. But in the days since, when she scarcely tolerated his presence and continually became prickly when speaking to him, he had started to doubt himself.

One minute, he adored the minx, and the next, she vexed him like the very devil.

Perhaps the stress of the moment had exaggerated his affection.

Or was he as fickle as a Saturday night harlot?

His self-reflection didn't exactly paint him in a flattering light.

Still, could Robyn be in love with Georgine, even if she could not tolerate him?

Was love that capricious?

And if this be-jumbled, perplexing, maddening conundrum was indeed that elusive, much-touted emotion, was he destined to suffer from unrequited love as had his friends Jack Matherfield and Shelby Tellinger?

Though neither man would ever admit that fact.

Besides, Jack had claimed his happily ever after when he married Aubriella, and Robyn strongly suspected Shelby and Roxina would march down the aisle in the not-so-distant future.

Taking a deep breath, Robyn crossed his ankles and folded his arms across his chest, willing Doctor Tinsdale to exit Georgine's chamber with an update.

Robyn's musing meandered back to his feelings toward Georgine—feelings he had taken great care to conceal—although Matilda might have guessed his secret.

Certainly, Robyn's interest in Georgine went beyond brotherly or platonic.

She utterly intrigued him, and not just because she was a founding member of the *Ladies of Opportunity* secret gambling society—a society he wasn't supposed to know about—but because she possessed strength, intrepidity, and an adorable stubborn streak most people missed.

He only knew about the *Ladies of Opportunity* because Mrs. Pottle, his former cook, had recently let something slip. Though long retired, he looked in on her, making sure she had plenty of coal and tea.

During his last visit, aware of her fascination with cricket, he had teased, "Have you been to any cricket matches of late, Mrs. Pottle?"

Delight lit her wrinkled face.

"Indeed, sir. I won a neat sum wagering the visiting team's bowler would send his first ball wide. I placed the bet through the secret gambling society operated by Aubriella Matherfield, Georgine Thackerly, and Claire Granlund—oh, merciful heavens!"

She had clapped a hand to her mouth. "I ought to have my tongue bolted tighter than a convent door. You weren't to know a thing about that, sir."

Winking, he leaned closer. "Your secret is safe with me, Mrs. Pottle. I shan't breathe a word."

And Robyn hadn't.

Yet.

He could imagine Georgine's surprise—perhaps affront and anger—if he did.

Yes, he would have to time that carefully.

Georgine had managed the small inheritance from her grandmother with skill and cleverness, all the while acting as a surrogate mother to Regina, ten years her junior.

A half-grin quirked his mouth upward on one side.

His fiery little betting bluestocking.

Someday, he would have a discussion with her about the intriguing enterprise she and her friends operated.

He squinted at the door again.

Did the doctor's extended examination portend unwelcome news?

Fiercely independent, Georgine would struggle to accept any diminished use of her arm.

What if—Robyn sucked in a ragged breath between his clenched teeth—*if* the infection becomes so severe, the doctor must remove the limb?

Queasiness curled up Robyn's throat.

Eyes closed, he said a rare and brief prayer on Georgine's behalf.

It could not hurt, and she needed all the help she could get.

Another twenty minutes passed before the doctor exited the chamber, his expression grim and mustached mouth tight.

Robyn straightened, trying not to appear too anxious or interested, when both sentiments pummeled him like a champion pugilist's fists. "Doctor...?"

"Miss Thackerly's wound has become putrefied—not severely but enough to cause me concern. I had hoped frequent bandage changes and the daily menu I prescribed would have strengthened her enough to prevent such an occurrence, but the chipped bone complicates her healing."

Sighing, the doctor rubbed his furrowed forehead with two fingers. "I shall need to check on her twice daily until the threat passes."

And if it didn't?

Robyn did not voice the question, for he knew the unpleasant answer.

Amputation.

Perhaps...*death*.

At the horrific thought, his stomach roiled again.

Steady on, Robyn Wade Gillson Fitzlloyd.

Don't tally your winnings before the dice have left your palm.

He forced his focus back to Doctor Tinsdale.

"What can we do?" He met the doctor's concerned gaze.

"I've applied a honey and garlic poultice to battle the infection. There is a jar of the poultice in her chamber. I want it, and the bandages changed every four hours. The old bandages and poultice cloths should be burned. Whoever changes the bandages must painstakingly wash their hands with soap, rinse thoroughly in clean water, and dry using a fresh towel. Every time. No exceptions."

He pressed his lips together. "Insist Miss Thackerly take nourishment, even if she isn't hungry. Especially the tonics I prescribed."

Easier said than done.

The good doctor had not experienced Georgine's obstinate side.

It didn't escape Robyn that she usually reserved that bit of her character for Robyn alone.

"She needs her strength to fight the fever and infection." The doctor removed his spectacles and tucked them into his jacket pocket.

What was it Robyn's mother used to say?

Starve a cold, feed a fever?

Neither of which made particular sense to him.

"Her sister is supposed to arrive tomorrow, and her friends have asked to visit her more than once." He cupped his nape again, trying to rub away the rocks that had gathered there from worry and tension.

So far, only Robyn, Matilda, and a maid had been permitted into the invalid's bedchamber.

"Her sister's presence might be helpful for an hour or two a day, if she isn't a chatterbox or flibbertigibbet. And only if she is in good health." The doctor cocked his head and then shook it. "But no other visitors. Miss Thackerly cannot be exposed to illness, and she needs to rest, not entertain. She also needs to be monitored around the clock for the next couple of days. If she worsens, fetch me at once."

That meant Robyn wasn't sleeping tonight, but then, he hadn't slept well since that godawful day in the garden. A recurring nightmare of Georgine being shot and dying woke him every night.

"Understood." Robyn gestured down the corridor. "Shall I see you out?"

"No." Doctor Tinsdale shook his head, the merest hint of a smile teasing the corners of his mouth. "I know the way."

He ought to.

He'd been here often enough, having been the Fitzlloyd family doctor for decades.

After the doctor retreated down the passageway, his footsteps fading into the house's stillness, Robyn slipped into Georgine's chamber. A fire burned low in the hearth, and a turned-down Argand lamp stood on the nightstand, its polished brass base gleaming in the soft glow. A tall glass chimney shielded the steady flame, casting warm, golden light across the rose-patterned walls and damask-draped bed.

"Robyn?"

Georgine's raspy inquiry tore at his heart.

"You should be sleeping, minx."

Offering a reassuring smile, he crossed to her, propped up on several pillows, including two to support her injured arm.

With the floral cotton chintz coverlet pulled up to her chin, she appeared small and fragile.

"I hurt too much to sleep." The thick rope of her plaited sable hair lay across her good shoulder, and she searched his face with her big sapphire blue eyes. "What did the doctor say?"

Just like Georgine—honest and direct.

"He said that you have a slight infection, and that you must rest and eat and drink *everything* he prescribed so you get well quickly. He also wants your bandage changed frequently and a fresh poultice applied each time, but I suspect that is exactly what he told you."

She didn't deny it, but instead wrinkled her nose. "I shall never be able to abide honey or garlic after this."

He chuckled as his gaze fell on a blue-gray book on the nightstand.

"Shall I read to you?"

She followed his gaze.

"Matilda brought it this afternoon. It is the first volume of Jane Austen's *Northanger Abbey* and *Persuasion*. I hadn't started reading it yet."

Though Georgine would bite off her tongue before admitting it to Robyn, she probably didn't have the strength to hold the book.

He had gifted the rare volume to Matilda last year, and it pleased him she would share the treasure with Georgine.

"Then allow me." Robyn pulled an overstuffed chair forward and, after turning the lamp up a bit, sank onto the plush cushion. He glanced up to find Georgine watching him, an enigmatic expression on her face.

What was she thinking?

He hadn't long to wait.

"You really should not be in my bedchamber without a chaperone, Robyn. As you well know, it is highly unseemly."

She had a point, and he could have asked a maid to sit up with her, but the truth of it was, Robyn did not trust anyone but himself and Matilda to nurse Georgine.

Worry creased her forehead.

To lighten the mood, he waggled his eyebrows and jested, "I shan't tell if you don't."

Even weak as a newborn kitten, she rolled her eyes at him. "As if *I* shall ever breathe a word of this scandalous arrangement."

He glanced at the clock and made a mental note of the time. Her bandages would need to be changed in four hours, and to preserve her delicate sensibilities, he would have to wake Matilda to attend to the task. "How is your pain?"

"The doctor insisted I take a dose of laudanum. He said that by managing my pain, I shall heal more quickly." Georgine curled her pretty mouth into a wry smile. "I detest the stuff, but it does make the pain bearable, and after he examined me, I needed a bit of relief."

Robyn bet she had.

"Robyn?"

He searched her pale face, noting with concern the pain pinching the corners of her mouth and eyes. "Yes?"

"Please do not tell Regina, Roxina, or the others about the infection. Regina will work herself into a proper dither, Roxina will blame herself, and the others will only fret. Ask Matilda not to as well, please." Despite her pain, Georgine summoned a fragile smile.

So like her to fuss about everyone else while she recovered.

"I would delay my sister's coming, but I fear Regina and Claire would become suspicious that something was amiss." Wincing the merest bit, Georgine tightened her mouth.

Throughout her ordeal, she had shown tremendous resilience and strength, never once complaining or dissolving into tears.

Robyn couldn't help but admire her fortitude.

"Matilda can keep Regina entertained." She would have to because having her sister flitting about would not help Georgine heal. "Can I get you anything before I start reading?"

Georgine licked her lower lip. "Can I trouble you for a drink of water? Not laced with laudanum this time, if you please."

Robyn chuckled.

"Of course." He swiftly poured half a glass from the decanter on the nightstand, then gingerly propped her up as she took a few sips, taking care not to jostle her injured arm.

The effort seemed to drain the last of her strength, and she sank back into the pillows with a ragged sigh.

After setting the glass on the stand, he collected the book.

"I have orders to monitor you *all* night." To lighten the statement, Robyn raised his eyebrows and gave her a mischievous smile, bracing himself for her objections.

Instead of getting ruffled and balking as he expected, she murmured, "Thank you."

Her quiet acquiescence alarmed him, but he kept his expression neutral.

Clearing his throat, Robyn opened the book. "*No one who had ever seen Catherine Morland in her infancy would have supposed her born to be an heroine.*"

Georgine closed her eyes, and not for the first time, Robyn

admired the thick lashes. Only now, they created a stark contrast on her wan cheeks.

Fifteen minutes later, he set the book aside, confident that the gentle rise and fall of Georgine's chest and the steady cadence of her breathing meant she had fallen into a fitful sleep.

He leaned forward, placing his elbows on his knees and resting his chin on his clasped hands.

"Why do you fascinate and haunt me, Georgine Thackerly?

"Of more import, what am I going to do about it?"

SIX

Rose Bedchamber
Fernleigh House

Four days later—early morning

Her limbs oddly heavy, Georgine slowly opened her eyes.

Where am I?

For a second, she didn't recognize the bedchamber, and alarm pelted through her. A moment later, last night's events tumbled into her memory. She remembered falling asleep while Robyn read to her, but she could not recall a dashed thing after that.

Had she slept through the night then?

The first time since she had been shot, although from the house's hushed stillness, she would guess dawn had not yet arrived.

Doctor Tinsdale's insistence that she take a dose of

laudanum seemed to have worked. She hadn't even roused when her bandages and poultices required changing.

Perhaps she had turned a corner for the better.

She felt almost her old self again—though her hunger raged unchecked.

At that precise instant, her stomach growled so fiercely it seemed as if her belly button were gnawing at her spine. She instinctively flattened her palm on her belly. Hopefully, the doctor would permit her something heartier than bone broth, milk toast, and gruel now.

"You are awake. Thank God."

Relief, edged with desperation, coarsened his voice to a gravelly rasp.

Robyn?

Slowly, fearing any sudden movement would cause agony to her wound, Georgine turned her head.

Elbows resting on his knees, he sat in the same chair he had last night. However, the man looked, in a word, wretched. Dark stubble roughened his jaw, while purplish shadows and lines of fatigue framed his eyes.

He truly looked fit for Bedlam.

Guilt for causing him another sleepless night assailed her.

Perhaps he was desperate to use the necessary and had been afraid to leave her, given the doctor's orders.

For heaven's sake. Why hadn't he rung for a servant if nature demanded immediate attention?

After glancing at the heavy, drawn draperies and assuring herself that no light filtered inside at the edges, Georgine puckered her forehead.

"It's not even dawn, Robyn."

A raspy chuckle escaped him, and he plowed a hand through his dark blond hair, something he had done often, given the strands stuck out in all directions. He had removed his neckcloth and waistcoat, rolled his shirtsleeves, and unbuttoned the top three buttons of his shirt, revealing an enticing glimpse of curly, dark blond hair.

She took his measure again. "Are you quite well?"

This was the first time she could recall seeing him disheveled and unkempt. Not that Robyn could be called a dandy by any means, but he did present himself as a gentleman, and the rumpled man beside her would be hard-pressed to pass as such.

What could only be described as a tender smile arched his full mouth, and his eyes glinted with amusement. Already handsome, when he smiled, he nearly blinded her. Not that *he* would ever know that silly fact.

Sensible misses—and Georgine was above all else sensible —did not act like ninnyhammers when men, particularly ruggedly handsome men, bestowed smiles upon them.

Their eyes locked, and for the life of her, Georgine could not tear her gaze away from Robyn's. A scintillating current buzzed between them, tangible and powerful, mesmerizing, and slightly disturbing too.

At last, he nodded, breaking the enthralling connection.

"I am now." Grinning, he rasped his hand over his bristly face. "You have been insensate and caused me—uh, I mean *us* —grave concern. I have been afraid to blink, let alone close my eyes for a spell. You miss," he shook a finger at her, "have caused a great deal of turmoil."

Perhaps too much laudanum had been administered to her.

That would explain her leaden limbs and moss-coated tongue.

Still, he needn't act so put upon.

"Really, Robyn." She glared at him, her dislike of being an imposition and unkempt herself, fueling her indignation. "I should think you would be pleased that I slept the night through."

He sat up straighter.

"You misunderstand, Georgie."

He never calls me Georgie.

"You did not just sleep through one night, but *four* nights."

"*Four*?" she whispered, glancing around the chamber.

It too, appeared rather a mess.

"Your fever rose dangerously, and you fell into a delirium and could not be roused." His tone carried a peculiar thickness, as if he could barely get the words past his tight throat.

What about Regina?

She jerked her attention back to him and spoke in a rush. "My sister. She must be frantic. Where is she? I want to see her."

He shook his head before speaking in a soothing tone, as one would to an overwrought child.

"Calm down, Georgine. She's still at home." He leaned forward and turned the lamp up, casting a golden glow upon the coverlet. "She sent word the day she was to arrive that she had contracted a head cold, and Doctor Tinsdale gave specific instructions that she should remain at home until she completely recovered."

"That makes sense," Georgine murmured, unable to dismiss the logic.

"He says your body does not need to battle anything else at present." He winked, and her stomach plopped over. And not from hunger. "I'll send a footman this morning with a note telling her you miss her."

He paused, giving her a cautious glance, as if he wasn't certain whether to continue. "Although she'll have to wait for the doctor's approval to come to Fernleigh House. Per your request, we have kept your battle with fever and infection from her."

Georgine gave a small nod. "I appreciate it."

Nevertheless, she could not quell a pang of disappointment.

She missed her sister, and truth be told, left to her own devices, Regina was wont to blunder into mischief or mishaps. It chafed that Claire should be put upon for so long, too. On the other hand, Georgine doubted she had the strength to supervise her young sister, and it galled her to further impose upon the Fitzlloyds.

The question that had been knocking about in her mind since she awoke could not be contained. "Why are you here and not Matilda or a maid?"

He leaned back in the chair, as nonchalant and at ease as a panther lounging on a tree limb.

"What, you are not thrilled by my attentiveness? My diligence and sacrifice?" He circled his hand in the air. "La, I believe I'm quite wounded."

The wily man deflected, but before Georgine could say as much, her stomach chose that moment to growl so loudly, Robyn's eyebrows shot ceilingward.

"Impressive." He contained a grin—barely—but couldn't quash the humor sparking in his nut-brown eyes. "A veritable lioness."

"I beg your pardon." A mortified blush heated her cheeks.

Lioness indeed.

At the moment, she felt distinctly more slothful.

"Let's see about getting you something to eat, shall we?" He rose and stretched, and despite her feeling as limp as yesterday's posies, Georgine could not help but admire his muscled physique.

"Thin gruel? Weak broth? Barely water?" She scrunched

her nose, trying to ignore the throbbing pain in her shoulder. Yes, she sounded ungrateful, and after fasting for four days, her stomach probably could handle nothing more substantial, but how she wanted to chew. "I would prefer something more palatable. A nice pudding or custard?"

"Not unless the doctor approves." The compassionate upward sweep of his mouth made her tummy flutter.

What in the world had come over her?

Hunger.

That was what.

She was famished. Lightheaded. Not able to think clearly.

Nothing else.

"How would you like a bath and your hair washed? You cannot get into a tub, of course, but I'm sure something can be arranged." He glanced at the wrinkled linens. "Fresh linens, too, I think."

The idea pleased Georgine so much, she couldn't contain her pleased smile or summon a jot of offense at the implication she might not be as fresh as one could desire. She would endure the pain and humiliation to be clean. "That sounds heavenly."

"Excellent." Robyn gave another brief nod as he turned toward the bellpull. After tugging on the cord, he added a couple of pieces of wood to the fire.

"I'm sure you shall want the chamber warm for your ablutions," he said by way of an explanation.

Georgine considered him from beneath her lashes.

Why had he stayed with her and not Matilda or a maid, which would have been more appropriate? He'd neatly avoided answering the question, and she was fairly certain that if she pressed him, he would do so again.

Why?

"Now that your fever has broken, I'll wager you'll be up and about in no time." He leaned a broad shoulder against the fireplace mantel. "Speaking of wagers, what is this ladies' gambling enterprise that you and your friends are involved with?"

Georgine's heart skipped a beat before accelerating.

How did he know about the *Ladies of Opportunity*?

Surely Matilda hadn't told her brother.

When Aubriella had invited Matilda to join their small troupe, she had emphasized secrecy and tact.

As the *Ladies of Opportunity* became increasingly known and more ladies took part in the discreet wagering, it only made sense that word would spread about the clandestine organization.

Still, that Robyn would boldly ask about it unnerved Georgine.

Georgine must speak with her friends about this as soon as possible. Until then, she must deflect without outright lying. She abhorred liars.

Canting her head, she shook a finger at him and affected a playful mien.

"That is not something I can discuss with you." She painted a pained expression upon her features—not a great stretch given the fierce ache in her shoulder—and affected fatigue and frailty. Again, easy to do. "Particularly given I've only just roused from a four-day stupor."

She let that point hit home.

At once, chagrin flashed across the sculpted planes of Robyn's face, although a hint of something steely lingered in his eyes, as if he'd guessed her game but let her win this round. "Of course. Please forgive my lack of sensitivity."

A moment later, a brief rap echoed upon the bedchamber door.

"Come." Straightening, Robyn angled toward the entrance.

A sleepy maid slipped in, probably having just risen herself. Uncertainty and worry creased her plump face until she noticed Georgine. At once, a relieved smile swept her wide mouth upward. "'Tis good to see you awake, miss."

"Thank you." What else was Georgine supposed to say?

"I'm utterly spent and scarcely fit for polite company," or *"I'm so fatigued, I might as well be pressed into the carpet?"*

The maid turned her attention to her employer.

"You rang, Mr. Fitzlloyd?"

"Yes, Nelly." Robyn rubbed his nose.

He appeared fit to swoon from sheer fatigue.

"Miss Thackerly is hungry. Cook knows what she can eat. Please bring a tray. She also wishes to bathe, wash her hair, and have the bed linens changed. Do you think those can be accommodated?"

"Of course, sir." Nelly gave an eager nod. "I shall make the arrangements."

"Also, please see if my sister has risen." Robyn covered a yawn with his hand.

The poor man appeared utterly spent.

"I need a bath myself, and I know Matilda wanted to know when Miss Thackerly awoke."

"I'll see to it at once, sir." With a little bob, Nelly practically dashed from the bedchamber.

Georgine tipped her mouth into a wry half-smile. "I'll bet she's sprinting down the corridor, skirts raised to her knees, to alert the house to my present state."

Not particularly keen on being the center of attention, Georgine found her current situation disconcerting for multiple reasons, one of which was the *Ladies of Opportunity.*

She counted on the funds from the wagers to help sustain her income.

Had her friends held meetings without her?

Had wagers been accepted?

Of course, they had.

And then there was Robyn's knowledge of their covert society.

Did he know Matilda had recently joined the *Ladies of Opportunity* as a board member?

Likely not.

Robyn would not approve.

As soon as Doctor Tinsdale agreed she could have visitors, Georgine would request that Aubriella, Roxina, and Claire call. Surely, they had wagering details to share with her.

She quite enjoyed the various clever wagers, and it never failed to amuse her how silly some were, although ladies seemed less inclined to bet which fly could walk up a pane of glass the fastest or the number of cats crossing St. James Street in one hour than men were.

Probably because women had much less coin to waste.

"I know you asked for your sister and friends not to know about the infection, but it was impossible to keep it a secret from the staff." Robyn gave an unapologetic shrug. "Doctor Tinsdale had them preparing many concoctions and poultices. It didn't take a sleuth to deduce your wound had become putrid. They were all tremendously worried on your behalf."

Georgine wasn't vexed, and, in truth, found their concern touching. "I was mainly concerned about Regina and my friends working themselves into a froth when there was nothing they could do."

"Poor Mittie." He chuckled, the sound resonating in his broad chest. "She has kept them informed of your progress, and more than once, she admitted, she almost gave the game away." He cast a fond glance toward the closed door. "My sister is not a master of deception. She's more apt to blab the truth accidentally, but she kept *your* little secret."

"I owe her my gratitude. For that and for attending to my care." Georgine stretched her calves. God, what she wouldn't do to rise from this bed. "I am confident she has been a diligent nurse."

Robyn's features softened. "She has, at that, to the point I insisted she go to bed before she collapsed from exhaustion."

Poor Mittie, indeed.

Another wave of guilt engulfed Georgine.

From his haggard appearance, she would guess Matilda wasn't the only one fagged to death. Again, she pondered why Robyn had avoided answering her question about why he monitored her. Assuredly, the impropriety didn't escape him, but there was naught to be done about it now.

Water under the bridge and all that.

"You do not have to wait for Nelly to return, Robyn."

Georgine sent a pointed glance toward the closed door.

"I'm not likely to expire before she returns. I realize I've been quite a burden to you. Please, attend to whatever you need to." She lifted her chin in a show of strength, although if he looked closely, he couldn't miss her slight trembling from fatigue. "I shall be fine. I am possessed of the constitution of an ox and the disposition of a lark."

The latter added a bit of levity, but Robyn didn't take the bait.

Hands on his lean, buckskin-covered hips, he gave her an indiscernible look from those warm brown eyes. "I have never said or indicated you are a burden, Georgine."

SEVEN

Fernleigh House Drawing Room

Several days later—afternoon

For the fourth time in forty-five minutes, Robyn stealthily paced past the open drawing room door. He glanced inside at his houseguest, content-as-a-cat-in-a-cupboard-of-cushions. Georgine appeared engrossed in the Jane Austen volume Matilda had loaned her.

Pure foolishness if you ask me.

All it takes is one slip, one little misstep, and Georgine might further injure her arm.

Hadn't Doctor Tinsdale warned about that very thing?

Indeed, he had—this morning, as a point of fact.

"A fall could permanently injure Miss Thackerly's shoulder. Once permitted to leave her bed, she must be accompanied by no fewer than two attendants, preferably male, so they can catch her if she starts to tumble—taking the utmost care not to jostle her arm and shoulder, of course."

Which, by God, could be better managed if Georgine weren't a pig-headed, mulish, feminine dervish, too stubborn for her own good and everyone else's. She became more headstrong and contrary each hour she remained confined to her bedchamber, and more than once in the past week, Robyn had gnashed his teeth in frustration.

She seemed hellbent on opposing him at every opportunity.

Today, Georgine had refused to stay abed or in her room, proclaiming she would go mad from inactivity and boredom.

Despite his misgivings about her leaving her chamber, empathy pricked Robyn. He wouldn't have lasted as long as she had. Idleness didn't mesh well with him, but *he* hadn't nearly turned up his toes a fortnight ago either.

Georgine, on the other hand, had escaped death by a hair's breadth, according to the doctor.

Did she understand how deathly ill she had been?

That reinfection or reinjury prolonged her stay at Fernleigh House, and the longer she stayed, the greater the chance her reputation might become smudged?

Tarnished?

Compromised?

Had *that* little detail that had worked her into a froth that first night here escaped her?

Robyn wasn't so stupid as to remind her of that pertinent fact...yet. They had been at odds this past week, and knowing Georgine as he did, she would likely demand a carriage be brought round and toddle herself home in a trice.

No, by God.

The mulish minx would insist on driving herself.

Nevertheless, wasn't she the one forever going on about

impropriety, appearances, her reputation, and all that rot? Well, perhaps not *rot*—the *haut ton* extolled men sowing their wild oats while casting a gimlet eye at any female who merely blinked wrong. Still, he'd heard Georgine's concerns so many times, he could recite them by rote.

Regina had offered to play whist in Georgine's bedchamber—a tremendous sacrifice for the flighty girl—but Georgine only shook her dark head.

"No. I am leaving this chamber. Today. Now."

For a moment, Robyn thought she might actually stomp her foot.

And now here she was, sitting on a once plush armchair covered in faded floral damask, with bastions of equally faded and worn cushions and pillows surrounding her...just in case.

Robyn felt no discomfort or embarrassment at Fernleigh House's aging and dated content. As long as things remained functional, what need was there to spend funds to replace them?

Who cared if the rugs had grown a bit threadbare or the wallpaper and tapestry were better suited to two or three decades ago?

He preferred the lived-in, time-worn comfort of well-used and well-loved furnishings. Not that he couldn't afford to refurbish if he desired.

He simply did not wish to.

If he married, his wife could tackle that task, if she so chose. In fact, his nonexistent wife could refurbish the whole blasted house—except for his study. That private, masculine oasis would remain just the way it was.

Oh, very well.

He might permit his wife to replace the draperies and carpets. Something Turkish would do.

The Fitzlloyds' wealth came primarily from importing and

exporting fine textiles, especially high-quality wool and cotton supplied to domestic and international markets. The booming demand for English cloth secured them lucrative contracts with mill owners and merchants. Robyn also invested in the East India trade, profiting from tea, spices, and other coveted goods.

Never let it be said that the Fitzlloyds skimped on their tea. Only the best would do.

Orange Pekoe, Imperial, and Flowery Congou.

Beyond textiles, he held interests in shipbuilding and maritime commerce, owning shares in merchant vessels that carried cargo across the Atlantic and throughout the British Empire. Though these ventures carried risks, they provided a steady income.

While they never rivaled banking dynasties or the great landed aristocrats, the Fitzlloyds' prudent financial management sustained a refined lifestyle, including a respectable household, well-bred horses, and occasional participation in the social season. Descended from gentility, they occupied the space between the traditional gentry and the rising class of industrialists.

It had never bothered Robyn that he didn't hold a title, though he claimed several titled peers as friends. The Fitzlloyds rubbed elbows with London's elite when it suited them, but did not aspire to anything loftier. *Smelling of the shop*, kept a few doors closed to them, but not many. Neither Robyn nor Matilda had any desire to associate with those snobs.

He knew little of Georgine's family, only that her father had died when she was a teenager, and her mother had gone to meet her maker two years ago. Not wealthy, Georgine and her sister survived on a small inheritance from Georgine's maternal grandmother—and that questionable gambling income from the *Ladies of Opportunity*.

Robyn allowed himself a few moments to observe Georgine covertly.

Color had returned to her cheeks, and the addition of solid food this past week had removed the hollows from her cheeks. Her sable hair, threaded with coffee-brown and molasses shades, shone in the afternoon light. She wore the luxurious cascade down, with a pale blue ribbon across her crown and tied at her nape.

All in all, she looked remarkably well—a lovely delicacy too pretty for mere words.

He narrowed his attention on her shoulder.

The infection had subsided, but her shoulder had a long way to go before completely healing, according to the doctor. And given the nature of her wound, the risk of reinfection lurked. Erring on the side of caution to ensure Georgine wasn't exposed to any illnesses, the *no visitors* order remained in effect.

That also worked well to help conceal her presence in the house, and although he had explained the delicacy of the situation to the servants, that didn't mean some of them hadn't blabbed.

Even the best, most loyal servants gossiped.

Not Bichard, the butler, however.

That man would cut his tongue from his head with a butter knife before revealing the smallest private detail about what went on in Fernleigh House.

Nonetheless, to be thorough, Robyn and Matilda had also not been home to callers.

Regretfully, that had not prevented Mrs. Verbena Wynecott from pounding upon the entrance door twice in the last fortnight, no doubt with her oversized ledger containing his and Matilda's pre-selected *volunteer duties* for her annual Charity Garden and Fancy Fair.

Mrs. Wynecott would extol what an honor it was to serve while delicately implying the previous year's donation was *just a touch modest.*

Last week, her loud objections to being turned away had carried upstairs. Robyn half feared the intrusive dame would shove past Bichard and march through the house until she cornered him or Matilda.

The woman bullied everyone, and not for the first time, Robyn wondered why Reverend Obadiah Goodfellow allowed Mrs. Wynecott to remain the charity's patroness.

"I can hear you, Robyn."

Georgine's irony-filled voice jerked him back to the present.

Feeling very much like a lad in a skeleton suit caught with his fingers in the bonbon dish, he stopped mid-step, peeking over his shoulder.

She continued to read, or at least she remained bent over the book.

Regina giggled and twisted on the settee to grin and waggle her eyebrows at him.

That one was a walking vexation, by God.

How Georgine dealt with her antics and larks, he could not imagine. Matilda spent half her time contriving entertainment and outings for Regina, and the other half caring for Georgine.

Matilda sent him a sympathetic smile before returning to arranging the flowers she'd picked this morning. No fewer than three vases held treasures from the garden.

Matilda's talent for growing things had developed beyond a mere hobby.

Robyn shifted his feet, and the floorboards squeaked.

"Oh, for pity's sake." Georgine sighed and laid the open book in her lap, spine up. She gave him an arch stare. "You're worse than a caged panther, Robyn Fitzlloyd. Either join us or take yourself off, so I can read in peace."

Rubbing his jaw, Robyn wandered into the drawing room.

For modesty, Georgine had draped one of Matilda's wrappers, a pretty thing fashioned from printed cotton with a delicate pattern of pale blue sprigs scattered over a cream background and indigo vines edging the hem and cuffs, over her nightgown.

Her comfortable attire hid the bandages, and a sling held her arm in place, ensuring her shoulder did not move. Given her restricted ability, maneuvering into a gown proved impossible, probably for several weeks to come.

Matilda tilted one last purple dame's rocket before stepping back to admire her handiwork. After giving a satisfied nod, she glanced at the inlaid brass mahogany clock atop the walnut fireplace mantel. "It's almost tea time. Regina, why don't you and I prepare the tray today? Every lady must know how, even if she has servants to wait upon her."

Robyn was quite sure Georgine had taught Regina how to prepare tea. The invitation was more to keep the girl occupied than a need to learn the skill.

Regina hesitated, gazing at Robyn with something akin to adoration.

Good God.

He kept the shock from registering upon his face, but only just.

Had the chit become enamored of him?

She couldn't be more than fifteen or sixteen.

Matilda must have noticed Regina's rapt attention too, for she hurried to grasp the girl's hand. "You may act as the hostess and help choose the dainties. I believe Mrs. Fennick baked jam tarts this morning."

That did the trick.

Regina bounced to her feet.

"I've poured tea at home, of course, but only with Georgine and occasionally a visitor." She sent Robyn a coy glance. "Never with a handsome gentleman in attendance."

Georgine raised an elegant eyebrow.

Ah, so she had noticed her sister's smitten behavior.

Matilda and Regina exited the drawing room, heads together as they discussed the proper procedure for nipping sugar from the cone.

Yes indeed, Regina Thackerly kept one on constant alert.

Robyn needed to nip Regina's infatuation in the bud, but how to do so without causing lasting hurt?

Perhaps he should seek Georgine's advice on the delicate subject.

Still, how did one broach the subject?

"I'm not an eggshell teacup in danger of shattering, Robyn."

Georgine tilted her head, roving her intelligent gaze over him.

"You needn't hover about. Go do whatever it is you do with your days. If I become fatigued, I shall return to my chamber." She twisted her mouth into an apologetic half-smile. "I vow the walls were closing in on me, Robyn."

He chuckled, pausing for a moment to smell a pale pink stock in the floral arrangement on the table between two tall windows. "Matilda possesses a deft hand with flowers."

"Yes, she truly does." Georgine's smile widened. "She is quite good with Regina too."

Nodding, Robyn perched on the settee's arm.

"I say, Georgine." He cleared his throat. "This is rather awkward."

"Is it about Regina?" She ran a slender finger along the book's spine.

Robyn gave a slow nod. "How did you—?"

"You've been sending me frantic glances like a man who's lost a duel with a blancmange."

She snapped the book shut and gave him her full attention. "Go on."

"Well… she appears to be under the impression that I am —how shall I put this?—an object of intense admiration." He tugged at his cravat. Discussing a teenage girl's infatuation proved decidedly off-putting, especially since Robyn quite fancied the elder sister.

Georgine leaned back, her expression amused. "She's sixteen. Last week, she was in love with Lord Byron. The week before that, it was a French waiter. Her *tendre* shall pass soon enough, I assure you."

Robyn lifted a shoulder. "She looks at me like I've written poetry and bled heroically for the crown."

"So, what do you propose?" Georgine fought a smile. "Fleeing the country? Feigning an incurable rash?"

What would Regina do if he declared himself to Georgine, admitting he was interested in courting her?

What would Georgine do?

Perhaps now wasn't the time, but soon.

Before Doctor Tinsdale released her to travel.

Head canted, Robyn crossed his arms. "I was rather hoping you might speak to her. Gently. Possibly while pretending I'm engaged to someone frightfully plain and fond of rectory records."

"I could claim you've sworn an oath of eternal celibacy." Hilarity shone in her blue, blue eyes and pulled her rosebud mouth upward at the corners.

Now she was making a May game of him.

Shaking his head, he gave an exaggerated wince.

"Too dramatic." And not likely this side of heaven, by God. "And that might only encourage her to reform me."

"Leave it to me. I shall be tactful." Georgine shifted slightly, as if to get more comfortable. *Northanger Abbey* and *Persuasion* toppled between the cushions encircling her chair.

"Drat." Bending forward, she giggled. "I cannot see the book. The pillows have swallowed it whole."

"Never fear, fair damsel. I shall retrieve your tome." Robyn shot her a grin. Bracing one arm on the chair, he kneeled to retrieve the volume. As the book had slid under the chair, the act nearly placed his head in her lap.

He glanced up, and their eyes locked.

At once, sensual tension engulfed him.

Georgine felt it too.

Her eyes rounded, then went soft and womanly before she darted her tongue out to wet her lips.

Robyn almost groaned out loud.

He'd wanted to sample that sweet mouth for weeks now.

Perhaps, one small kiss...

"Georgine..."

Voices and footsteps sounded in the corridor.

Deuced unlucky timing.

To ease the strain, he quipped, "Matilda and Regina prepared the tea tray in record time."

Georgine cleared her throat, and when she spoke, her voice had a husky tenor. "Perhaps you should wait until I have returned to my bedchamber."

"Not a bit of it. Almost there," he grunted, straining further, his cheek brushing her thigh.

God help him.

"It's wedged fast, Georgie."

"I didn't realize it would be so hard…"

A theatrical gasp sliced through the air. "*Scan-dal-ous.*"

<h1 style="text-align:center">EIGHT</h1>

Still in the drawing room

Half a dozen awkward seconds later

Robyn froze.

Bollocks.

Several more, even fouler curses paraded through his mind.

He knew *that* voice.

Of all the drawing rooms in all of London, she had to walk into his, just now.

"I am correct in surmising Matilda and Regina have not returned with tea?" he whispered.

"You are," Georgine murmured, her eyes wide as she peered past him.

Bracing himself, Robyn glanced over his shoulder.

As he expected, Verbena Wynecott, attired in lavender from her garish feathered bonnet to her bombazine gown and spencer, clutched her black ledger to her ample bosom and gaped at him, aghast.

And if he weren't mistaken, slightly titillated as well.

She rather resembled a beached bass, gasping for air, and her eyebrows, graying, wiry things, cavorted about her forehead like drunken caterpillars.

With considerable effort, he wrestled his grin into submission and schooled his face into a banal mien.

Mehetabel Twigg, Mrs. Wynecott's long-suffering companion, as timid, thin, and dowdy as Mrs. Wynecott was intrusive, stout, and garish, hovered near her employer's elbow.

Miss Twigg braved a shy peek through her eyelashes before slamming her focus to the floor.

Crimson skated up her cheeks as she fidgeted with her reticule's strap.

"I beg your pardon, Mr. Fitzlloyd." Bichard pinned Mrs. Wynecott with a condescending glance. "Madam would not listen when I explained you were not at home to callers."

Mrs. Wynecott was so high in the instep, she was likely to trip over her own consequence. Besides, other than tackling the woman—and probably losing the wrestling match—what was Bichard to do?

"You may go, Bichard." Robyn dipped his chin. "Please check on Miss Matilda and Miss Regina and the preparation of the tea tray."

"Very good, sir." The butler nodded, and after glowering at the dame again, retreated.

"Good afternoon, Mrs. Wynecott, Miss Twigg." Robyn stood, and acting like it was perfectly normal to be found on his knees before a lady, brushed off his trousers. The dashed book would have to wait. "How fortuitous. You are just in time for tea."

Mrs. Wynecott *always* timed her arrival to partake in tea.

She set upon a bountiful tea service like a wolf on a Sunday lamb.

"Matilda should return any moment with the tray." Robyn adjusted his coat sleeve, taking a moment to half-turn and wink at Georgine before facing Mrs. Wynecott again. "I believe she mentioned Cook baked fresh jam tarts."

Mrs. Wynecott couldn't quite conceal her little "O" of delight, and Miss Twigg blinked her owlish eyes as if she could not quite believe her ears.

When was the last time the poor woman was permitted such a treat?

Recovering from her momentary excitement about the tarts, Mrs. Wynecott directed her buggy-eyed gaze at Georgine. She peered down her substantial nose before speaking in her haughtiest and most disapproving tone, though avid curiosity glittered in her eyes. "I do not believe we are acquainted."

Blast and damn.

To suggest Mrs. Wynecott was a chinwag of the worst sort was an exaggerated kindness. She could concoct a scandal from a sneeze and a sideways glance.

There was no help for it, however.

Robyn forced a congenial smile as he made the introductions. "Mrs. Verbena Wynecott, may I introduce Miss Georgine Thackerly, our house guest? Miss Thackerly, this is Mrs. Wynecott, and her companion, Miss Mehetabel Twigg."

Not quite the proper thing as far as introductions went, but they would suffice.

Miss Twigg darted an apprehensive glance at her employer but forged ahead. "My friends call me Hetty."

Saints be praised.

Had Miss Twigg grown a backbone at last?

"Sounds like a hen pecking." Mrs. Wynecott's unkind

comment brought another furious blush to Miss Twigg's cheeks.

"It is a pleasure to make your acquaintance, Hetty," Georgine murmured kindly, discarding protocol and acknowledging the companion before her employer.

Bully for her.

She'd just declared herself Miss Twigg's friend, and from the grateful look Miss Twigg bestowed upon Georgine, she had earned lifelong devotion.

Georgine curved her mouth into a gracious smile as she carefully pushed her hair off her injured shoulder. "And your acquaintance, too, Mrs. Wynecott."

Georgine would not have said that if she knew Mrs. Wynecott. The matron's mind made a full chamber pot seem pleasant, and her tongue wagged faster than a racehorse ran.

"*Hmph.*" Mrs. Wynecott sniffed before narrowing her eyes and prying. "*How* exactly are you related to the Fitzlloyds?"

Angling her head, Georgine offered another sweet smile, but a jot of annoyance sparked in her irises.

"We are not relations, just friends." She gestured toward her injured shoulder. "I am recovering from a gunshot wound."

Polite, but to the point.

"*Gunshot?*" Mrs. Wynecott's beetle-bug eyes grew impossibly rounder as she stared unabashedly at Georgine's sling.

No doubt the snoopy old biddy was dying to ask the details, but even she wasn't that brazen.

"And you chose to convalesce here, Miss Thackerly?"

And that tidbit would gallop through the *ton* faster than a husband-hunting debutante chasing an eligible duke.

"I had no choice. I was shot in the garden." Georgine's smile became as brittle as dried leaves. "My physician insists that I would have died had I been moved. Therefore, the

Fitzlloyds graciously opened their home to me and my sister as I recover."

Take that, Mrs. Wynecott.

"But, my dear." Mrs. Wynecott tutted, affecting false camaraderie. "Your reputation..." Her tone became conspiratorial. "Surely, you must have a care what others might think —the conclusions they may draw."

Mrs. Wynecott didn't fool Robyn.

She practically frothed in anticipation of spreading this *on dit.*

"Which is why we are *not* at home to callers." Robyn let his point sink home, but as always, Mrs. Wynecott paid no mind to anyone but herself.

Like a schooner in full wind, she sailed to the settee.

As she and Miss Twigg settled onto the cushions, the decades-old piece of furniture groaned in protest. The portly woman leveled a superior look at her slender companion. "Perhaps you should abstain from dainties for a time, Miss Twigg."

Miss Twigg's jaw sagged as she sent a not-so-covert, incredulous glance toward Miss Wynecott's ample girth, the generous rolls straining against the fabric.

Robyn couldn't prevent his bark of laughter, which he disguised as a cough by pressing his hand to his mouth and hacking dramatically. "Pardon me. Happens every spring. Must be something in bloom. Think it might be the dogwoods."

He coughed again, just for effect.

Georgine suddenly found a pillow's silk fringe utterly fascinating.

Robyn swore her lips twitched as she too wrestled to keep her mirth in check.

"What I mean to say, Miss Thackerly," Mrs. Wynecott

leaned forward and waved a hand up and down toward Georgine. "You are in a state of dishabille, and Mr. Fitzlloyd was practically lying in your lap. Even *I*, who takes the greatest care not to jump to assumptions, must admit I was taken aback. The scene I came upon smacked of scandalous impropriety."

She elevated a caterpillar eyebrow. "One might mistake you for...*paramours*."

Her last word came forth as a singsong hiss.

Only someone with a tosspot for a brain.

Georgine tilted her head and delivered another of her sweet smiles, something Robyn had learned meant she was about to send a dart to target. "*Fama, malum qua non aliud velocius ullum.*"

And we have a bullseye.

She had quoted from Virgil's *Aeneid*.

Robyn wanted to applaud.

Furrowing her broad forehead, Mrs. Wynecott looked to Robyn, then Georgine, and finally to Miss Twigg as if she weren't positive if she had just been insulted, but suspected she had been.

Evidently, Mrs. Wynecott did not speak Latin.

"It is a quote from *Aeneid* by Virgil, Mrs. Wynecott. '*Rumor—an evil than which no other is more swift.*'" Miss Twigg lifted her chin and met her curmudgeon of an employer's gaze head-on. "It means gossip or hearsay becomes more exaggerated, distorted, or sensational the more it spreads."

Yes indeed, the mouse had found her squeak—and rather a sharp one, at that.

"I *know* what it means, Miss Twigg." Mrs. Wynecott inhaled an affronted breath, her chins quivering in outrage. "I did not come here to be insulted."

She stood, the epitome of offended snootiness, and pressed her ledger to her chest.

"I regret to inform you, Mr. Fitzlloyd, that St. Winifred's Charity Garden and Fancy Fair does not have volunteer opportunities for either you or your sister this year."

Praise God and all the saints.

She leveled a blistering glare at Georgine.

"Nor your *houseguest*. If that is what you choose to call her." She gave a disdainful sniff. "Though the evidence suggests something *far* more improper."

"My attire reveals far less of my form than does yours, Mrs. Wynecott." Georgine regarded the infuriated woman unflinchingly. "Perhaps you should have the seams let out— several inches."

Miss Twigg smiled, but quickly subdued her humor, lest her overbearing employer notice.

All pretense of geniality gone, Mrs. Wynecott pointed and wagged a thick finger between Robyn and Georgine.

"A Christian fundraiser cannot be associated with immoral and dissolute conduct." She speared Robyn a self-righteous glare. "Have you no thought for your sister's reputation, sir? To carry on with your mistress under the same roof?"

Devil take it.

Too bloody far.

He shot Georgine a swift glance.

She appeared composed, but he saw the hurt shining in her blue eyes.

"How unfortunate." Knee cocked, Robyn placed a hand on his hip. "I am equally penitent that I shall not be donating to the charity this year. Or in the future."

Daggers shooting from her eyes, Mrs. Wynecott pressed her lips together so tightly, they resembled a goose's hind end.

"I vow, I shall inform Reverend Goodfellow. Such blatant and wicked behavior calls for excommunication."

If that were true, half of England's church pews would sit empty on Sunday mornings.

Robyn had had enough of the woman's insolent behavior.

He flashed her his most charming smile, all the while condemning her to Hades with a blistering stare. "Did I mention I shall be making a *very* generous donation to St. Winifred's? It is *your* fundraiser that I want no further association with."

St. Winifred's Church wasn't such a wealthy parish that Obadiah Goodfellow would look a gift horse in the mouth, and from the sour expression contorting Mrs. Wynecott's face, she knew it. "We shall see. There are *other* ways of dealing with the likes of you. I vow, you shan't be putting on airs then."

A threat if Robyn had ever heard one.

And one, the malevolent harridan would not hesitate to act upon. Which meant, Robyn had just waded into shark-infested waters and dragged Georgine with him.

He had best come up with a solution and swiftly.

Drawing herself up, Mrs. Wynecott jutted her chin out. An unfortunate act, as it exposed two long black whiskers, which appeared to compete for length and stiffness. Radiating sanctimonious propriety, she stomped toward the door, causing several gewgaws to rattle on the marble-topped tables they rested upon.

"Come, Miss Twigg. I refuse to spend another minute in this house of *sin*."

A muffled gasp carried into the drawing room, followed by indiscernible muttering, though Robyn clearly heard "purple cow" and "tale-peddler."

Bichard, no doubt—fiercely loyal but prone to eaves-dropping.

Miss Twigg defied her employer and slipped closer to Georgine. Voice lowered, she murmured, "I would like to place a wager with the *Ladies of Opportunity*."

She darted a nervous glance over her thin shoulder, and relief flooded her features upon realizing her infuriated employer had tramped into the corridor.

"May I call another time? When you have recovered?" She clasped her reticule. "If I win my wager, I shall have enough funds to leave her employ. With her sour looks and sourer tongue, she is enough to curdle cream, and I've had quite enough of her unkindness."

"Of course, Hetty." Georgine laid a hand on the woman's arm. "I shall inform the other members. If you cannot get away, just send a note around with the bet. We can collect the funds another time."

"Excellent." Hetty beamed.

Georgine returned her grin. "May I ask what the wager is?"

Hetty glanced nervously at the door again. "Mrs. Wynecott has been skimming off the charity donations for years. That's all I can say for now."

"Miss Twigg!" Mrs. Wynecott bellowed. "If you wish to remain in my employ, attend me at once."

"I don't, but I must. For a little while longer." With a little flutter of her fingers, Miss Twigg dashed from the drawing room.

"That woman..." Georgine sucked in a large breath, then slowly released it, shaking her head. "If I never lay eyes upon that creature again, it will be too soon. She is utterly vile."

Georgine had only glimpsed the smoke, not the fire.

And Robyn had to protect her from the raging inferno that was sure to come.

Hell, how was he supposed to tell her?

Robyn scraped a hand through his hair.

"We have a problem, Georgine."

"Oh. And what is that?" She tilted her face to meet his eyes, and he vowed he saw admiration in their depths. "I think you did a splendid job of ridding the house of that maggoty potato."

Clearly, she did not understand what was about to happen —what Mrs. Wynecott could this very instant be setting into motion.

Though he applauded Mrs. Wynecott getting her comeuppance, the woman was malicious beyond measure. "She is a known rumormonger. She will, without a doubt, shred your reputation."

"Let her. We know the truth, as do those I care the most about, and that is enough for me." Georgine shrugged. "It sounds like her good name is about to become smudged, though she deserves what is coming to her."

"No, Georgine. I fear you do not understand the full scope of the situation." Robyn shook his head. Because Georgine didn't have an evil mind, she couldn't grasp how despicable another person could be. "It's far more complicated than that. Mrs. Wynecott will fabricate...things."

"What could she possibly say, Robyn, and who would believe her if she is the gossip, you say she is?"

Disgusting, abhorrent things he was not about to voice to Georgine.

"Even a whiff of a scandal could ruin all of you." He had to make her understand how grave their predicament had become. "You and Regina will be shunned. Ostracized. Matilda, too."

Women always bore the brunt of rumors.

Georgine chuckled, and at another time, Robyn would

have relished her throaty laugh. "Because of a mean-spirited gossip? Surely you exaggerate."

Robyn sucked in a long breath.

Who could have guessed when he got out of bed this morning how sharply the day would veer off course?

Bloody hell.

How had everything gone to rack and ruin faster than a debutante's virtue at Vauxhall?

He'd considered courting Georgine to test the waters, so to speak. Now, however, in the suds up to his cravat, he would have to skip the wooing piece and leap straight into a marriage proposal.

God help him.

And Georgine.

"There's no help for it, Georgine.

"We shall have to get married.

"Immediately."

NINE

Still in the drawing room

After ten or fifteen painfully slow tick-tocks of the mantel clock

"*Married?*"

Georgine gaped at Robyn as if he wore boots upon his ears.

She closed her mouth with an audible snap.

Really.

Had he taken leave of his senses and packed them off to Bath?

"You. Cannot. Be. Serious."

She shook her head a tad too vigorously, and her shoulder twinged in protest.

"I do not wish to cause offense, Robyn, but I absolutely am not tootling down matrimony's lane because of a nasty chinwag. In truth, I have never wanted to marry."

Georgine could summon any number of reasons for becoming snared in the parson's mousetrap, but trotting down the aisle for fear of tattle someone *might* spread?

No, thank you.

Still, she'd never seen amiable, easy-going Robyn so, well... in high dudgeon and frothing like a teapot on the boil.

In truth, she had never witnessed him in a pelter before.

She couldn't deny his genuine concern, but to conclude marriage was their first option?

Flimflam and fiddle-faddle.

"Come, Robyn. Be honest. You do not want to marry any more than I do."

Her words sounded harsher than she had intended.

The edges of his mouth and eyes flexed the merest bit at her bluntness. "I've always intended to wed someday."

"What I mean is, neither of us is interested in an arranged marriage. Of course, you will marry." He would make an excellent husband. Just not hers. "Someone you choose because you love her."

His features remained unchanged, but something flashed in his eyes and disappeared before she could identify it.

"I agree an arranged marriage is not ideal, but believe me, Georgine, there *are* worse things."

Robyn shoved aside the fashion periodicals strewn on the tea table and sat upon the polished surface. Such earnestness creased his handsome face as he leaned forward, his elbows on his knees, that for the first time, a sliver of genuine alarm sluiced through her.

God above.

He is absolutely serious.

And that frightened the stuffing out of her far more than peering down the barrel of a gun had mere weeks ago.

Marriage was forever.

Women seldom escaped unhappy unions, and once they said, "I do," they became little more than chattel, forced to bend to their husband's every whim and desire.

If they didn't?

Well, some men—men like her dead father—did not hesitate to inflict their will with their hands.

She had seen the bruises Mama tried to hide.

Suddenly feeling quite like a bird in a snare, Georgine shot a glance toward the entrance.

Where were Matilda and Regina?

Did they have to milk a cow for the tea today?

"Georgine. Are you listening?"

Robyn scrubbed a hand down his face.

The poor man was truly in a dither.

"Mrs. Wynecott saw you in your night attire." He acted as if Georgine had been caught nude.

"Because I am recovering from a wound." No one could fault her for that.

"Exactly. Flushed. Disheveled. Alone with me..." He let out a short, humorless laugh. "And I was on my knees."

"Retrieving a book I dropped." Georgine lifted her good shoulder. "Perfectly innocent."

"That's not what Mrs. Wynecott saw." He gestured vaguely to the room. "Or rather, not what she chose to see. And when you delivered that brilliant set down..."

In Latin, no less.

"Because she has a filthy mind." Georgine bit her lower lip.

Mayhap she *had* been a touch too quick to offend the woman.

No.

No, she had not.

Mrs. Wynecott hadn't hesitated a jot to impugn her. "And she went on to call me your mistress."

Her cheeks burned hotly upon saying the words.

As if she would ever agree to be any man's mistress.

Robyn's mouth thinned. "Which she is now likely repeating to every gossipmonger within a twenty-mile radius."

"But Robyn, as I've already said," Georgine adjusted her sling to ease the increasing ache in her shoulder. "If she is known as a horrid gossip, *who* would believe her?"

"Half the *ton*, I expect. The other half won't need to. The image alone—me kneeling before you, you in your nightdress, flushed and breathless—it will be more than enough."

"I was not breathless." Perchance a little flustered at having a man's head so near her lap.

A perfectly natural reaction.

"I doubt Miss Twigg will risk dismissal quite yet." Genuine remorse shadowed Robyn's face and darkened his eyes to a deep coffee. "She'll remain silent, which will only add substance to Mrs. Wynecott's fabrication."

Only too true.

Companion positions were as scarce as invitations to Almack's Assembly Rooms—something Georgine had never received and was not likely to. Not that she desired an invitation.

"I was surprised by her barging in unannounced and uninvited. It flustered me." It seems Mrs. Wynecott appeared precisely where she was least desired, much like a gale sweeping in from the Channel—only louder. "That is why I appeared flushed."

"Society does not care a snap." Robyn snapped his fingers; the sound loud and oddly startling.

A tiny morsel of doubt crept into Georgine's mind.

He brushed a finger over her cheek.

"They never do. The truth is dull, Georgine. Scandal, on the other hand, spreads like fire through dry thatch—and no one bothers to ask where the spark began or who started it."

She opened her mouth to object, but couldn't.

Every word rang with truth; more was the pity.

Anger simmered inside her at the injustice.

What a horrid bumblebroth.

"Facts are far too plain for their ignoble tastes." She twisted her mouth in derision, not caring that she sounded bitter. "They crave scandal—juicy, sordid, and preferably ruinous."

"Yes." Robyn sighed, the sound hollow and resigned. "It is a fault of humankind."

"Not all humans. Some refrain from such vileness." She stared past him, idly noting the breeze teasing the purple lilac blossoms outside the window. "Matilda and Regina *will* suffer because of the scandalmongering."

He had already said that.

So dashed unfair.

She had said *that* already too.

"They can put aside all hope they have of making a match." He lifted her good hand and cupped it in his palm. "They'll be turned away from drawing rooms, receive cut directs, and their names will be whispered behind fans. Yours will be dragged through the mire."

Georgine couldn't prevent her involuntary flinch, and Robyn must have seen it because he gently squeezed her fingers.

"I cannot stand by and allow any of that when I can prevent it," he said softly.

Gossip drew blood as surely as any blade, the wounds lingering long after the whispers faded.

He brushed his thumb over her palm, the movement soothing and tantalizing at the same time.

"Georgine, I know this isn't fair. We've done nothing wrong. But this is how Society works. And the only way to salvage this mess is to alter the story to our benefit. We shape the truth into something palatable."

The intensity in his warm brown gaze made her heart beat faster and sent a rush of sensation flooding through her.

Only Robyn had ever caused her to respond in such a feminine manner.

"And we must act quickly before Mrs. Wynecott paints something grotesque and irreparable." A steely edge had entered his voice.

She narrowed her eyes, not yet willing to concede her freedom for the trappings of matrimony. "And I suppose you have just such a solution?"

"In fact, I do." He winked. "Something rather clever, I think."

There was the boyish charmer she knew so well.

"And?" Georgine lifted her eyebrows. Even as she asked, in her mind, she railed against the injustice.

No, no, no.

I do not want to hear his solution.

I shall not like it. I shan't.

"It's quite simple, but I believe it will hold up under scrutiny." The contours of Robyn's face folded into thoughtful lines. "We fell in love during your convalescence and are secretly betrothed."

Love?

Betrothed?

She studied him, as taken aback by his lack of rancor over their situation as she was by his quickly contrived scheme.

Why didn't he seem distraught about his proposition?

Wouldn't a man resist being forced into a marriage with

the same intensity as Lucifer would, compelled to attend a baptism?

Especially since she brought nothing to the union but a high-spirited sister and a small stipend?

Oh, and thanks to Mrs. Wynecott, a tainted reputation and questionable virtue.

Oblivious to Georgine's internal argument, Robyn continued, "We decided to wait until you had recovered to share our good news with our family and friends—and to pick a wedding date."

Plausible, but would their sisters and friends believe the taradiddle?

Regina would.

Anything to do with romance made the girl dreamy-eyed, though she might have her feelings hurt because Robyn didn't return her regard.

Georgine eyed Robyn from beneath her eyelashes.

He had come up with a plan, and a trifle too dashed quick for her comfort. But then again, this situation was beyond the pale and called for extreme measures.

"I do not like lying." She pursed her mouth. "It's not an ideal foundation for *marital bliss.*"

Georgine couldn't keep the scathing sarcasm out of her tone.

Was she considering his offer?

How could she?

She could bear the sordid tattle, whispers, and sly glances —the snubbing too.

But Regina...

She was the social butterfly and a romantic at heart as well.

Georgine was not.

Too young to remember their father's abuse, Regina regarded love and marriage with an innocent's fairytale ideals.

Would that she-devil's forked tongue truly destroy any chance of marriage for Regina?

Robyn hesitated, something other than vexation darkening his brown eyes. "If I thought there was another way... But I shan't allow your name—or our sisters'—to be dragged through the muck."

Good God.

Marriage.

To Robyn.

"What say you, Georgine?" His tender smile made her heart trip over itself. "I promise to be a good husband and father."

Father?

Sweet Jesus on Sunday.

How had he jumped to *that* already?

She still struggled with marrying him, let alone sharing a bed and giving birth to his children.

For the first time in her life, Georgine acknowledged she might become a mother.

Before she could respond, Matilda flew into the room, panting, as if she had sprinted the length of the house. Face pale and features taut, she wrung her hands together.

Robyn jerked his head up, instantly alert.

"What has upset you so, Matilda?"

Georgine had never seen Matilda in such a state.

"Robyn, Nelly just took me aside." For an instant, Matilda appeared about to cast up her accounts. She pressed both palms to her stomach.

Something drastic must have happened, and Georgine prayed it had nothing to do with the walking scandal sheet in stays who had departed this room only minutes ago.

"Mittie?" Robyn gently coaxed. "What did Nelly say?"

"As she returned from her half-day off, Nelly overheard

that boiled cabbage in a bonnet, Mrs. Wynecott, blabbing to Lady Brammall and Mrs. Peasonhaugh down the street that she came upon you and Georgine in…"

Closing her eyes, she swallowed.

This was not good.

Not good at all.

Georgine's stomach twisted into a tight knot as she braced herself.

So much for answered prayers.

"*In what*, Mittie?" Steel threaded Robyn's gentle question, reminding Georgine of the unyielding and rather ferocious man in the garden weeks ago.

Slowly, Matilda opened her eyes.

Regret and embarrassment shone in their depths.

"In *congress*." She choked on the word before blurting, "With the drawing room door wide open for the world to see."

Robyn swore beneath his breath.

"*Bloody hell.*"

"Oh, my God." Georgine buried her face in her good hand. "She's Satan's slithering spawn bedecked in silk and slippers."

"Georgine, we must marry."

Georgine slowly lifted her face, taking in Matilda's horror.

"And we must do so immediately." Urgency inflected Robyn's voice and face. "There is no time to delay."

Georgine tore her attention from Matilda's mortified face. She could not let her or Regina suffer from what that devil's doxy would do with her false accusations and slanderous lies.

Her heart and throat aching, she lifted her chin, determined to be strong, though she felt she might dissolve into a weeping, wailing mess any second.

Nevertheless, she forced the dreaded words past her stiff lips.

"Very well, Robyn. I shall marry you."

She steeled her emotions and her resolve.

This might not be the path she had chosen for her life, but heaven help her, she would determine the pavement she walked upon.

"But I have terms."

TEN

Fernleigh House Drawing Room

Three days later—half of eleven

Robyn glanced up from studying the flickering sunrays on the faded Aubusson carpet.

After two days of pouring rain, the sun had battled through the pewter clouds, almost like an omen of good things to come, or as a blessing on this special day. Because no matter the circumstances, marrying Georgine marked the day as special in his memory for all time.

Appearing staid and solemn as always, Reverend Goodfellow stood near the unlit fireplace, holding a well-used volume of *The Book of Common Prayer*. The black calfskin prayer book contained the vows Robyn and Georgine would soon exchange.

Georgine entered the drawing room, sandwiched between Matilda and Regina.

Both appeared far happier and radiant than Robyn's bride.

At Georgine's behest, only their sisters would act as witnesses to the brief ceremony.

Robyn had expected she would want the other *Ladies of Opportunity* present, but had honored her request. He hadn't even invited his cousin, Shelby Tellinger. Shelby would demand an explanation, and once given, would understand.

Because of her arm's limited mobility, Georgine still could not wear a proper gown.

Matilda and Regina had surprised her with a pretty new wrap.

The champagne-colored silk wrap shimmered as it clung to Georgine's shoulders, its folds shifting with every step. Silver thread outlined delicate vines along the edges, and periwinkle blue forget-me-nots bloomed in each corner. Celadon green tassels swayed at the front, anchoring the wrap in place with effortless grace.

One sister had swept Georgine's hair into a simple but elegant Grecian updo.

Someone, likely Matilda, had also tucked a few orange blossoms in Georgine's hair.

She wore no jewelry, but in her good hand, carried a nosegay of pink-striped peonies, delicate lily of the valley, soft pink dianthus, and pale blue love-in-the-mist. A thick white satin ribbon encircled the stems.

Her humble wedding attire caused a poignant lump to lodge in Robyn's throat.

No wonder she did not want others in attendance.

Not only was Georgine entering a marriage of convenience, but what bride wanted to exchange vows in her nightclothes with her arm in a sling?

She should have been draped in satin and lace, dripping in

jewels, and carrying an enormous bouquet that rivaled the church's floral decorations. All of their closest friends and acquaintances should have been there to mark the joyous occasion after the banns had been read for three weeks.

Afterward, the guests would have been treated to a sumptuous feast, and she would have honeymooned in Italy or Greece or some other exotic location.

Instead, their wedding would be a brief—*very brief*—ceremony by special license, followed by a modest luncheon as Georgine's diet remained somewhat restricted.

For certain, consummating the marriage would have to wait.

Robyn wasn't a monster or so eager to bed Georgine that he would risk injury to her healing shoulder. Besides, every instinct he possessed bellowed for him to tread softly and take things at a snail's pace.

Let her come to him.

He was a patient man.

What was that old French adage?

"Tout vient à point à qui sait attendre."

All comes in good time to those who know how to wait.

And then there was Georgine's short list of terms.

No intimacy for at least six months—Robyn wouldn't have agreed to a marriage in name only, but he could abstain for six months.

Unless Georgine decided *she* wanted to become his wife in truth sooner.

Regina could attend Blenstock & Handcastle Academy for Young Ladies, if she desired, and then have a Come-Out Season—both acceptable provisions.

The wedding vows were to be as brief as possible—just enough to be legal.

Reverend Goodfellow had objected, and strenuously too,

until Robyn promised to replace the church's well-worn and often repaired fifty-year-old hymnals.

And finally, Georgine would continue with the *Ladies of Opportunity*—to which Robyn had agreed with the condition that she explain precisely how the organization worked.

As expected, she had balked, but eventually, she conceded to disclose the bare essentials.

And she had done so.

Formed by Georgine and her three closest friends, the *Ladies of Opportunity* oversaw a female-only betting book, much like White's. They operated with the strictest confidence, refused cruel bets or those that were ruinous, kept immaculate records, and the founders shared a predetermined portion of the bank.

Those details would suffice for now.

Robyn would have no secrets between them.

He knew full well that the only reason Georgine had conceded to marry him was to save their sisters' reputations.

She didn't give a fig about hers—or his, for that matter.

They had that in common, as well as their mutual concern for their sisters.

Georgine had said she had never wanted to marry.

Why?

Most young women, Matilda being no exception, dreamed of the day they would take a husband.

His less-than-subtle interrogation of his sister had yielded little useful information about the Thackerly sisters or their parents.

Matilda remained admirably—and a jot vexingly—tight-lipped about Georgine.

Mayhap one day Georgine would trust Robyn enough to share her reasons for resisting nuptials.

Her gaze collided with his across the room.

No joy or love glimmered in her blue, blue eyes.

Resignation, resolution, and determination, yes.

But also, desolation.

She does not want this.

If he had taken a dagger to the heart, the pain would not have been worse.

Robyn's anguish was not for himself, but for her.

He had promised to be a good husband to her, but a marriage of convenience to a reluctant bride made for unstable underpinnings for any union.

Damn Verbena Wynecott to the lowest level of hell.

How soon would *her* embezzlement be exposed to the world, and then she would suffer the consequences of her perfidy?

Not soon enough to satisfy Robyn.

No repercussions that Hades' handmaid endured sufficed for the harm she had inflicted on others for years.

With pure doggedness, he shoved all thoughts of the spiteful dame to a corner of his mind and focused on his bride-to-be.

Even pale and unsmiling, Georgine's beauty remained unmatched.

The moment seemed surreal.

Today, Robyn would take a wife.

A gorgeous sable-haired, sapphire-eyed spitfire bluestocking.

A reluctant grin kicked his mouth upward on one corner.

Life would never be boring; that was certain.

The Reverend cleared his throat. "Shall we begin?"

Panic flashed across Georgine's delicate features, and for a moment, Robyn thought she would turn tail and bolt.

Hugging her, Regina whispered something in her sister's ear, and Georgine's expression transformed from dread to resolve. Swallowing, she nodded, and with admirable poise, crossed to stand beside Robyn.

He smiled down at her, and she offered a tremulous upsweep of her lips in return.

After opening *The Book of Common Prayer*, Reverend Goodfellow flipped a few less-than-crisp pages until he came to the page he sought.

"Though it is unusual to have such an abbreviated recitation, we shall skip directly to the actual avowals. Please face each other, join right hands, and repeat after me."

Georgine passed her nosegay to Regina before extending her hand.

Robyn clasped the delicate appendage within both of his.

Her pulse beat a frantic staccato at her collarbone and beneath his fingertips.

She focused her attention on his chin, and Robyn fought a grin.

His bride-to-be was far from unaffected, and he couldn't help but admire her composure.

After glancing between them, Reverend Goodfellow began.

"Will thou Robyn Wade Gillson Fitzlloyd have this woman as your wife?"

"I will." Robyn did not hesitate.

This might not have been how he envisioned getting married, but there was no other woman he would rather have taken as his wife.

"Will thou Georgine Emily-Jane Edwina Thackerly have this man as your husband?"

Georgine parted her lips.

Would she?

Robyn held his breath.

She flicked her gaze upward, searching his face.

What did she seek?

"I will."

Firm. Steadfast. Clear.

They recited the binding vows in a blur, and then Reverend Goodfellow said, "The ring, please."

Robyn fished around in his coat pocket for a moment before extracting the thin, gold band—elegant simplicity.

He slid it on Georgine's finger.

Her eyes widened in surprise, and her pupils contracted to a pinpoint.

Had she thought he would not give her a ring?

Later, when she recovered, if she desired, she could select another, more lavish wedding ring. But somehow, Robyn didn't think she would. Though she liked pretty things, from what he had observed of her over the years, she preferred understated elegance.

Reverend Goodfellow concluded in a flourish, "Those whom God hath joined together let no man put asunder. I pronounce that they be man and wife together, in the name of the Father, and of the Son, and of the Holy Ghost. Amen."

"Amen," everyone murmured.

Beaming, her eyes bright with youthful excitement, Regina tucked her arm into the curve of Matilda's elbow. "We are truly sisters now."

"Indeed, we are." Matilda gave Robyn a bright smile. "And now you have a brother too."

A not-so-subtle hint that Regina would have to put aside any romantic notions she may have harbored for Robyn.

The reverend retired to a table, upon which sat the leather-bound parish register. "Mr. and Mrs. Fitzlloyd, Miss Thackerly, Miss Fitzlloyd, I shall need you to sign the register."

He held up a turkey-feather quill.

Mrs. Fitzlloyd.

That had a wonderful ring to it, despite the circumstances.

Using dark gall ink, Robyn signed the register's creamy page first, swiftly followed by the women.

Once done, he clasped Georgine's good elbow.

"Mrs. Fennick has prepared a festive luncheon for us." He winked. "I have it on good authority that there might be syllabub topped with fresh raspberries."

"That sounds delicious." A tiny spark ignited in Georgine's eyes, and though minuscule, it gave Robyn hope.

Regina had been all too eager to share Georgine's favorite foods, and her favorite desserts were syllabub and raspberries.

Her favorite flowers—lilies.

Favorite color—white.

Nevertheless, he had much to learn about his new wife.

He extended his arm toward the doorway. "Shall we?"

Never one to turn down a free meal, Reverend Goodfellow made a beeline toward the corridor, followed by Regina and Matilda, still arm in arm.

Robyn turned Georgine to face him and stared into her luminous eyes.

"We shall be happy, Georgine. I promise."

"Would you care to bet on that, Robyn?"

She raised a winged eyebrow, her mouth twisted into a humorless smile. "Or are the odds too risky?"

He leaned near to whisper in her ear, but her subtle perfume—*sweet pea, lily, and orange blossom?*—hit him with the impact of a freight wagon. He closed his eyes and gritted his teeth to rein in his raging desire.

Once he wrangled his passion under control, he grinned and winked.

"I'll take that bet, Mrs. Fitzlloyd. Name your terms, my spirited bluestocking."

She leaned away, the merest hint of a smile playing around the edges of her mouth.

How he longed to kiss those sweet, plump lips.

"I shall have to think about it, but be warned, I never place a bet I cannot win."

ELEVEN

Fernleigh House garden

Six weeks later—early in the morning

Georgine lifted her face, breathing in the perfumed air and enjoying the slightly cool and refreshing breeze. If today were anything like the past week, it might be too warm to venture outdoors this afternoon.

She didn't mind.

Not only was early morning her favorite time of day, but July was her favorite month. So many trees, plants, and flowers bowed beneath a bevy of blooms, and occasionally, she spotted a baby animal or bird. Plus, she enjoyed the abundance of fresh local produce.

She skimmed her gaze over the grounds.

Matilda had transformed the manicured space into a vibrant sanctuary, and it had become Georgine's favorite place at Fernleigh House. It didn't even bother her that the garden was where she had been shot.

How long ago that seemed.

How much had changed.

Indeed, how much *she* had changed.

Now that she was free to roam the house and grounds at will—Doctor Tinsdale had lifted several restrictions, so long as she didn't overexert herself—she sought the privacy and serenity the gardens offered.

She vowed she healed faster just being outdoors, surrounded by nature.

The doctor cautioned her to take care if she took trips to town or church, or attended gatherings, concerned that her healing arm might get jostled. He estimated it would be another two to three months until she fully healed, and only then would they know to what extent, if any, the damage to the bone had reduced the use of her arm.

Before this, she had never considered what recovery from a gunshot entailed.

Georgine didn't mind the extended convalescence now that she could move about Fernleigh House's grounds. She had no desire to enter the feeding frenzy that was Polite Society, particularly as hers and Robyn's names were yet on many flapping tongues.

Aubriella had shared that unfortunate and rather chafing detail during her last visit.

Old tabbies, bitter spinsters, and on-the-shelf wallflowers needed something to chat about, after all.

Georgine's friends came to call often, and they held the *Ladies of Opportunity* meetings here, the last on the garden veranda.

That reminded Georgine.

She wanted to speak with Cook and make certain the

lemon shortbread, almond macaroons, and marmalade puffs she had requested for tomorrow's meeting, along with finger sandwiches, would be ready.

Hetty had called three days ago and wagered every cent she had scrimped away during her employment with Mrs. Wynecott—fifty-one pounds. Her wager was quite simple. "Mrs. P shall be removed from all charitable committees of St. Winifred's before the quarter's end."

Hetty deserved her happiness and freedom from the harpy.

Pausing beside the ornate five-tiered fountain with its cheerful cherubs, Georgine trailed her fingers in the cool, burbling water. A bashful frog launched itself from behind the spout's dark recess, splashing into the largest scalloped basin.

"Hello there." She bent forward.

What a cute little thing, with those enormous black eyes.

"I shan't hurt you."

"Have you taken to talking to chubby stone cherubs, my dear?"

Since marrying, Robyn rarely addressed Georgine by her name, instead using terms of endearment.

Darling. My sweet. My dear.

And in private, even *my love* and *sweetheart.*

Georgine rather enjoyed the tenderness. It made her feel cherished, and that was a unique experience for her. No male, assuredly not Father, had ever made her feel precious and secure.

In truth, unexpectedly and much to her surprise, she rather enjoyed being married to Robyn.

Thus far, he'd been the epitome of kindness, patience, and attentiveness. If she didn't know he had been forced into the union, she might be fooled into believing he cared for her as much as she had finally admitted she cared for him.

How could she ever have considered him her nemesis?

Well, perhaps nemesis was too harsh a term, but troublesome and bothersome were not.

Was it only now, with her guard down, that she allowed herself to see him through undistorted lenses?

She still hadn't decided on the terms of her bet with him because the truth of it was, she had no desire to wager against their happiness. She wanted to embrace it, treasure it, see it grow into something meaningful and magical.

"Or are you talking to yourself again?" Robyn teased.

"I do not talk to myself, as you well know." A half-smile played around her lips. At one time, his teasing would have irked her. Now she found his roguish charm endearing and amusing. "No. It's a little frog. We frightened the starch out of each other."

"A frog, you say?"

"Come see." She half-turned and held out her damp fingers. "He or she is a little thing. I think it's a baby." Glancing over her shoulder, she asked, "How did you find me?"

Robyn chuckled, the sound rolling over her like a soft silk wrap. "When I couldn't find you in your bedchamber, I assumed you had asked Nelly to help you dress and made your way to the garden. It's where you usually are in the morning."

"How astute of you." Robyn had ordered several new gowns for her—all with front buttons and laces, since Georgine still couldn't lift her arm high enough to have a gown slide over her head. A condition, Doctor Tinsdale had warned, might be permanent.

It was bad enough that Robyn had been forced to marry her, but to be stuck with an invalid...Georgine kicked that ugly thought to next month.

The sky-blue and white striped morning gown she wore,

with its ruffled sleeves and hem, and embroidered ribbon encircling her waist, made her feel pretty...desirable even.

The appreciative glint in Robyn's eyes as he raked his intense gaze over her caused a little thrill to zip along her veins. Not so long ago, his intense scrutiny would have peeved her. That was *not* her reaction these days.

No, indeed.

"I had no idea I was marrying a morning sparrow." He bent and kissed her forehead. "I confess, I quite like it. I, too, enjoy the early hours."

That was something else he did—dropped kisses on her crown or forehead or cheek, but never tried to do more. And the truth was, she very much wanted him to do more.

Much more.

And acknowledging that didn't shock her as much as it would have mere weeks ago.

This past month and a half, as they'd spent time together, she'd discovered she not only liked Robyn—a lot—but he stirred feelings she wasn't quite certain what to do with.

Except she wanted him to kiss her.

That much she knew beyond a doubt.

She took a step nearer to him on the pretext of flicking a piece of lint from his lapel.

A very wifely thing to do.

He smelled marvelous: sun-dried linen and Castile soap, with the faint crispness of starched cloth and a whisper of bergamot from the pomade in his freshly brushed hair. And sandalwood, of course.

Had someone bottled masculinity, rakishness, and charm?

She inhaled deeply, savoring his essence.

As usual, a sensual shiver raised bumps on her arms and caused her tummy to quiver.

"Where is your froggy friend?" he asked in a husky purr.

God help me.

"It's just there, tucked into that niche."

Goodness, her voice had become positively sultry.

Something that caught her off guard and happened far too often lately. When exactly had he gone from being a pebble in her shoe to the comfort she never sought but could not now forgo?

Robyn winked as if he guessed her secret as he bent to inspect the little frog. "It is a tiny thing. Definitely a juvenile."

He was so close, she could see the gold flecks in his iris, and a little mark on his firm chin where he must have cut himself shaving.

His attention dipped to her mouth.

Did he want to kiss her too?

Yes. Yes. Please do.

He raised his gaze to hers, a question in his rich brown depths.

She parted her lips, but words escaped her.

How did one ask one's husband to kiss them?

Georgine had no practice at flirting. There had never been a need to attract a man's attention deliberately before. Nevertheless, attending dozens of balls, soirees, and routs had given her ample opportunity to observe ladies using their guile, subtle machinations, and posturing to entice gentlemen.

She leaned nearer until only a couple of inches separated their mouths.

There, that ought to do it.

Unless the man was as obtuse as a pumpkin.

Even so, Robyn hesitated.

What more of an invitation did he need?

Surely, he didn't expect *her* to kiss him.

And why not?

Marshaling every ounce of courage she possessed,

Georgine closed the distance and pressed her lips to his—the merest wisp, no harder than the brush of a butterfly's wing.

At once, Robyn cupped her nape and deepened the contact, something near a growl echoing in his throat.

"There you two are."

Georgine sprang away, her cheeks on fire.

Robyn bent toward the frog.

Wearing a cheerful pink and yellow floral morning gown, and oblivious to the scene she had just interrupted, Regina skipped toward them, the curls framing her face bouncing. "Matilda wants to know if we would like to accompany her to Bond Street today?"

Unlike Georgine, Regina adored shopping, even if she only selected a new ribbon for an old bonnet.

"We could stop at Gunter's Tea Shop for a lemon or strawberry ice afterward." Features animated, Regina looked between Robyn and Georgine.

Georgine hadn't indulged in a raspberry ice since before their mother died.

Regina looked so hopeful that Georgine hesitated before uttering the no that sprang to her lips. Neither Regina nor Matilda had ventured out since the wedding either.

"I think that's a marvelous idea. I shall accompany you. I would rather enjoy an orange ice." Grinning, Robyn shoved a lock of hair off his forehead. "We shall present a united front, and if anyone dares to give us the gimlet eye, we shall cock a snook at them, one and all."

Brave words.

He put his thumb to his nose in a comical gesture.

"What say you, Georgine?" His expression softened. "We shan't go if you do not feel up to it."

Georgine glanced at her sister.

Regina's big, pleading eyes tore at her resolve.

Half child, half young woman, Regina needed the outing. Georgine couldn't keep her hidden away at Fernleigh forever. At some point, they must venture out and face the wagging tongues and pointed glances.

Lifting her chin, Georgine nodded. "I need new stockings, and in this heat, Gunter's would be a treat indeed."

She had plenty of mended stockings, but a new pair wouldn't go amiss for a special occasion.

"That's my brave darling." Approval radiated from Robyn's eyes. Then, to her utter astonishment, he brushed a kiss across her lips, right in front of her sister.

And Georgine couldn't summon a scold for his impertinence, for her lips glowed hot from his touch.

Regina giggled. "I shall inform Matilda."

About the kiss?

No, ninny. About the outing.

With a flip of her wrist, Regina skipped away, calling in a sing-song voice, "Don't be long, you love birds."

The faint mist from the fountain cooled Georgine's hot cheeks.

Robyn stood close enough that the warmth of his nearness seeped through her gown. For weeks, they had spoken with careful politeness, their rare touches only the brush of fingers or the fleeting press of his lips on her forehead in a restrained farewell.

But now his scorching gaze held hers, steady and searching, as though weighing some silent question. The garden remained oddly still, save for the fountain's gentle splash of water and the rustle of leaves stirred by a soft morning breeze. A thrush trilled somewhere in the hedges, its song bright and unguarded, and Georgine's pulse beat in time with it.

Reluctant to break the spell, she slowly pivoted to return to the house. "I should go in too."

"Not before I kiss my wife in the manner she deserves."

When Robyn bent toward her, she told herself it would be another brief caress, no different from before. He looped a muscular arm around Georgine's waist, taking the utmost care not to bump her injured arm. With his other hand, he lifted her chin.

The moment his mouth found hers, all such expectations dissolved.

He moved his lips over hers with a tender insistence, deepening the kiss until the fountain's murmur, the bird's song, even the flowers' fragrance surrounding them faded, until there was only Robyn and her.

Heat unfurled within Georgine, curling low and sweet, each breath drawn against his mouth sending a shiver through her. She wrapped her fingers around his lapel, seeking an anchor as the world narrowed to the sure, unhurried passion of his embrace—and the wonder that, at last, she had stopped wishing for his kiss and now experienced it.

And deep within her, Georgine knew her life had irrevocably taken another turn.

TWELVE

Gunter's Tea Shop
Regent's Park - Berkeley Square

That same sultry afternoon

No one is staring or whispering—excellent.

Sitting beneath the striped cream and forest green awning jutting over Gunter's Tea Shop windows and shading the patrons from the blazing sun, Robyn and the women waited for their ices. Alert for the merest sign that anyone recognized him or Georgine, he surveyed the genteel crowd as he tapped his fingertips atop the pale cream iron-framed table.

If Georgine hadn't been recuperating, he would have initiated an outing weeks before. The delay in entering the public arena suggested guilt to those eager to spread more lies.

However, the postponement didn't concern him overly much.

Introducing Georgine and himself as blissful newlyweds

to a few carefully selected elites, and soon, Mrs. Wynecott's ploy to destroy them would wither like a nosegay left to the mercy of July's unmerciful sun.

Satisfaction thrummed through him, not because he was spiteful or vengeful, but because actions and choices had consequences, and he suspected Mrs. Wynecott, once a pillar of High Society, was about to get her well-deserved comeuppance and topple off her high horse, straight into infamy.

Yesterday, when Robyn delivered the bank draft to cover the cost of the new hymnals to Reverend Goodfellow, the usually staid man had been in a dither. So much so that he had taken Robyn into his confidence—a rare occurrence and one which revealed the man of God's distress.

Mere days ago, St. Winifred's churchwarden had received an anonymous tip: Mrs. Wynecott hadn't been entirely forthcoming about her fundraising, and the entries in her ledger differed from the actual donations.

Robyn would bet his reputation that Miss Mehetabel Twigg was the nameless source, and she had evidence to support her claim. Motivated by self-preservation, Miss Twigg had too much integrity to make such a bold accusation without proof.

Though the warden had only contacted the first few patrons recorded in the fundraising ledger to verify their contributions, according to the reverend, a disturbing pattern had emerged.

Apparently, Mrs. Wynecott stole a portion of every contribution and recorded the remaining sum. It appeared she had been doing so for several years with no accountability.

Had no one thought to audit her before now?

Embarrassed by his lack of oversight, the mortified man of God swore Robyn to silence until the investigation had been completed. In short, however, Verbena Wynecott would soon become the pariah of Society she had sought to make Georgine.

Justice well served, by thunder.

Robyn couldn't summon a jot of compassion or sympathy for the woman.

Georgine laughed at something her sister said, drawing his attention.

His heart burgeoned with emotion.

Steady on, old chap.

He was worse than a besotted youth experiencing his first infatuation. Only what Robyn felt for his wife went far beyond youthful captivation.

Far, far beyond.

He loved Georgine. Adored her. Cherished her.

Once he had admitted the truth to himself, his entire perspective on their marriage—his life—changed. And if he lived to be one hundred, a bald, hunch-backed, toothless codger, he would never tire of gazing upon her.

Even when time robbed her of her silken skin, sparkling blue eyes, shiny hair, and fetching smile. His memory—no, his soul—would forever be engraved with the woman now sitting across from him.

Until this morning, he hadn't dared to believe she might return his regard. But that kiss...

Their kiss by the fountain suggested something altogether different.

Up to this point, he had been content to love her without being loved in return, but now...?

He could not take his eyes off her.

Seemingly undisturbed by the oppressive heat, in a particularly fetching seafoam green gown, trimmed in cool white lace and ribbons, Georgine nodded at something Matilda said, causing the jaunty white marabou feather on Georgine's bonnet to bob.

Occasionally, someone noticed the sling cradling her arm, but after a cursory glance, directed their attention elsewhere.

She seemed oblivious to the few curious looks, or if she had noticed, disregarded them.

Her poise never failed to impress him.

The joy on her face and their sisters' made the outing worthwhile, despite the day's unrelenting warmth.

Waiters in smart bottle-green livery, cream waistcoats, and buff breeches moved briskly between the shop, tables, and carriages while skillfully balancing trays laden with molded fruit ices, plates of delicate sponge biscuits, and tall glasses of water ice.

Grateful that no uncomfortable encounters had ensued, Robyn allowed the tension knotting his shoulders to ease and curved his mouth into an easy grin.

A slight breeze ruffled the plane trees' leaves and carried a mingled aroma of horse, leather, baking confections, and the faint citrus tang of lemon and orange ices.

His attention dipped to Georgine's pink rosebud mouth.

He could still taste the sweetness of her lips, could still feel the jolt of pleasure her innocent, inexperienced response triggered as she kissed him back.

She kissed me back.

His soul fairly sang for joy.

A sharp kick to his shin jerked him back to the present.

Refraining from rubbing the abused appendages, he met his sister's amused glance.

"What was that for, Mittie?"

"You are staring at Georgine like a love-struck buck, and people have begun to notice," Matilda murmured while fiddling with the silver spoon atop a crisply folded napkin. "Take a look around, brother dear."

Robyn casually perused the crowd, smiling as several gawkers swiftly averted their attention.

He leaned back. "She is my wife. I am entitled to stare."

"Oh, you..." Matilda rolled her eyes, but he was saved from further censure as a handsome young waiter arrived with their ices and served her first.

Forehead puckered, Georgine looked between them. "Did I miss something?"

"No, nothing of import." Matilda spooned a bite of strawberry ice into her mouth. "*Mmm.* Delicious. We should do this more often."

If it would bring a radiant smile to Georgine's face, Robyn would pull the carriage to Gunter's himself.

"Enjoy, miss." The young man gave Regina a rakish smile as he placed her ice before her, and she practically melted into a pool at his feet.

"Fitzlloyd?" Robyn glanced upward to see Quinten Honeybrook with Claire Granlund on his arm, wending their way through the tables.

Since when had those two begun spending time together?

Granted, they often attended the same functions, but Robyn had never noticed either had a particular affinity for each other. In fact, widowed young, Claire Granlund usually presented a cold shoulder to any man who came within five feet of her.

Wed to a much older man, hers hadn't been a happy union, according to Georgine.

"Honeybrook." Robyn stood and doffed his fawn-colored felt top hat. "Mrs. Granlund."

"Please accept my felicitation on your marriage."

Honeybrook's smile didn't quite reach his eyes. In truth, the taciturn fellow seemed a bit distracted.

"Thank you," Robyn and Georgine murmured in unison.

"Claire. I cannot tell you how much I appreciate your help with Regina in those early days of my recovery." Georgine extended her good hand, and Mrs. Granlund grasped her gloved fingers.

"Think nothing of it, dearest. It is wonderful to see you have ventured out, Georgine." Mrs. Granlund nodded to Matilda and Regina. "I see you are enjoying an ice. Perfect for a hot day like today."

"It is." Regina popped a spoonful of lemon ice into her mouth as she not so covertly searched for the attractive waiter.

Robyn would have to keep an eye on the girl.

Matilda had never been a flirt, but Regina was a miss in pursuit, batting her eyelashes at everything in pantaloons under the age of thirty.

Robyn glanced between Honeybrook and Mrs. Granlund.

How long had those two been keeping company?

The tension radiating between the two was palpable.

Not a romantic outing, he would be bound.

What then?

Georgine noticed too.

Head tilted, she eyed Claire, a question in her eyes and a crease between her eyebrows. "I'm surprised to see you taking a stroll in this heat."

No doubt she was just as astonished to see her friend with Honeybrook as Robyn was.

Mrs. Granlund twirled her parasol, a dainty confection of pale ivory silk with scalloped stitching and whitework embroidery around the edges. "I would not dare without a parasol."

She did not elaborate, raising Robyn's suspicion further,

and from the slight tightening of Georgine's mouth, hers as well.

"We shan't keep you." Honeybrook doffed his hat before extending his arm toward Mrs. Granlund.

She hesitated a fraction too long before placing her gloved palm on his forearm, not linking her elbow with his.

Interesting.

Georgine met Robyn's gaze, and he read the silent question in her eyes.

What was that about?

Mindful they weren't alone, he lifted a shoulder as he turned to watch Honeybrook and Mrs. Granlund's progress.

They turned down Bruton Street.

Even more fascinating.

Honeybrook's solicitor's offices just happened to be along that very lane.

Georgine turned her attention to her ice, taking a dainty bite of the raspberry confection.

Robyn lifted his spoon and froze.

Hell's clanging bells.

THIRTEEN

Still at Gunter's Tea Shop

An impossibly uncomfortable heartbeat later

From the corner of his eye, Robyn caught sight of Mrs. Wynecott, wearing ruffled puce from head to toe and resembling an overripe plum, barreling toward them, a second before she trumpeted her arrival at the auditory expense of Gunter's unfortunate and unsuspecting patrons.

So much for avoiding unpleasantness on their outing.

"For shame, Mr. Fitzlloyd. Flaunting your mistress in public and in the company of your sister and Miss Thackerly's as well. It's beyond the pale." She plowed to a stop two feet from their table, her expression smug and superior, pure venom flashing in her eyes as she fanned her red, sweaty face.

Miss Twigg was nowhere to be seen.

Lucky her.

Several women, including Matilda, gasped, and a few

pulled their skirts closer as if fearful of Georgine contaminating them.

Robyn did not doubt that every eye bore into them, and fury billowed within him.

Georgine froze with her spoon halfway to her mouth.

Shock and horror darkened her eyes to navy blue.

Regina's jaw dropped, and her spoonful of lemon ice plopped onto the table, immediately melting into a sticky pool.

Robyn fisted his hands against the disturbing urge to grasp Mrs. Wynecott by her thick neck and shake her until all the feathers fell off her bonnet. Before he could give the cow the tongue-lashing she deserved, a familiar voice echoed over his shoulder.

"Fitzlloyd, you old rascal. I heard you had taken a beautiful bride. I suppose we shall forgive you for not inviting us to the wedding. I cannot blame you for wanting to keep her to yourself. I was of the same mind when I wed."

Maxwell, Duke of Pennington.

Robyn glanced behind him, delighted to see Pennington and several other peers. All leveled Mrs. Wynecott scathing glowers. 'Twas a wonder she remained standing under their scornful scrutiny.

Never in his life had Robyn been more grateful for titled friends. He didn't know or care what had brought the lot to Gunter's at this precise moment—probably on their way to White's Club—but their arrival was nothing short of a godsend.

If Verbena Wynecott thought to take the field against these peers, she ought to think again; a fat goose at Michaelmas stood a better chance of survival. Several were known for their sharp tongues and intolerance for stupidity.

Sucking in a sharp breath, Mrs. Wynecott paled, uncertainty flitting across her broad face.

Good.

She should be apprehensive.

Standing noble shoulder to noble shoulder and presenting a united front, several aristocrats stood a few feet behind Robyn. Besides Pennington, the Duke of Harcourt, the Earls of Renshaw and Wainthorpe, and Viscount Sethwick regarded Mrs. Wynecott with utter disdain.

Robyn rose and bowed. "Your Graces. My lords."

If their audience had been rapt before, now the patrons stared agog, their coveted ices forgotten and melting in the July heat.

"Come, old chap. Introduce us," the Earl of Renshaw urged.

He winked at Georgine before leveling Mrs. Wynecott a blistering stare that would have sent a more astute woman running with her tail between her stout legs.

Mrs. Wynecott was not astute, or else she would have concealed her thievery better. Obtuse, intrusive, and meddlesome, the dame continued to stare while sweating like a racehorse.

A flurry of introductions commenced, the peers waving Georgine and the sisters back into their chairs when good etiquette dictated that they rise.

The onlookers whispered among themselves, some likely never having encountered so many peers at once. There would be many exaggerated stories told around the dinner table and in drawing rooms tonight.

Most would not paint Mrs. Wynecott in a flattering light.

Despite that, the woman did not budge an inch.

By Jove, she had the brass for it—to stand there and smile as though she had not a thing to answer for.

Wainthorpe turned his black stare upon her. Many a man had cowed under that ebony glare. "I do hope I misheard you, madam, for besmirching the good name of our friend and his bride might be considered social suicide."

"Indeed," Harcourt murmured, his steely stare unyielding and unforgiving. "One should carefully weigh the words one speaks, particularly when they are pure fabrication."

Mrs. Wynecott licked her lips and glanced around. Few people regarded her with anything other than contempt. "I am privy to information—"

"I doubt you are on intimate terms with either Fitzlloyd or his wife." Renshaw scraped his hooded gaze over her, leaving no doubt he found her wanting. "And what you *think* you know means nothing. What *we* know..." he swept his hand toward the other aristocrats, "is that Robyn Fitzlloyd is an honorable gentleman and a man of impeccable integrity. Who are *you* to impugn his honor?"

"I...I..." she blustered and flapped her fan with such vigor, one would think she meant to sail the channel.

Robyn covered Georgine's hand and gave it a reassuring squeeze.

She straightened her spine, pinning Mrs. Wynecott with a look that would have frozen the Thames. "Leave. Now. And never, ever approach me or my family again. And before you sully others, perhaps you should take care that *your* behavior is beyond reproach."

"Indeed." A half smile arching his mouth, Pennington tugged on his earlobe. "St. Winifred's warden paid my wife a call recently. It seems there are discrepancies between what individuals have donated for the Charity Garden and Fancy Fair fundraisers the past several years, and what the church actually received."

A feline grin of satisfaction split his face. "Aren't *you* in charge of that charity?"

A buzz erupted among the spectators.

Likely, at one time or another, a few of those enjoying ices today had been approached by Mrs. Wynecott to donate.

Mrs. Wynecott visibly sagged, the wind having gone out of her sails. Without a word, she turned and, with her head down, wended her way from the enthralled crowd.

Harsh whispers and insults followed in her wake.

Thief. Charlatan. Judas.

Robyn almost felt sorry for her.

Almost.

He turned his attention to his friends. "Georgine is still recovering, but once the physician gives the all clear, we intend to have a reception. Of course, you are all invited."

To Georgine's credit, she maintained her poise at his heretofore undisclosed revelation.

They had never discussed having a reception, but once the idea took root, Robyn became convinced it was just the thing to establish their marriage and erase any remaining smudges from their reputation.

"Excellent. I shall inform my wife." Harcourt nodded. "I have no doubt she will be as delighted as I to accept the invitation."

The others murmured their agreement.

Regina, silent as a terrified mouse until now, perked up.

"A fete. Oh, I do love planning a party." She glanced at her sister. "Do you think we can have ices and sorbets, and Chinese lanterns, and...?"

Georgine gave her a tolerant nod while patting her hand.

"We can discuss the details later, dearest." She tipped her mouth into a pretty smile. "We will send the invitations soon."

Robyn hadn't expected her to agree to his impulsive declaration, let alone collaborate with him.

"I fear we must take our leave or risk being late for a meeting at White's, Fitzlloyd," Renshaw doffed his hat. "A pleasure to meet you, Mrs. Fitzlloyd."

The others echoed his sentiment before shifting toward the lane.

Robyn eyed his melted ice. "What say we go home and come for ices another day, one a trifle less hot?"

Nodding in agreement, the women rose.

Robyn tucked Georgine's hand into his elbow as they strolled behind Matilda and Regina toward the waiting carriage.

"Forgive me for putting you in a fix about the reception." Chuckling, he adjusted his hat to better deflect the sun. "The notion popped into my mind, and I spoke without thinking."

She angled her head so that their eyes met.

"Honestly, I think it is a grand idea, Robyn."

"You do?" For one so opposed to marrying, this turnaround was unexpected, though heartily welcome.

"I do." Pink tinted her cheeks, but the brave darling pressed on. "I want the world to know we are happily married and ours is not just a marriage of convenience or an arranged marriage."

He lowered his head, and her perfume teased his nostrils. As always, his body reacted with primal urgency. "Do I dare hope that you regard me with a small degree of fondness?"

This was not the place for such a conversation, but he desperately wanted to know.

They were nearly upon the carriage.

The driver had already assisted Matilda and Regina inside.

Georgine regarded him with soft eyes.

"More than fondness, Robyn."

FOURTEEN

Georgine's bedchamber
Fernleigh House

Nine days later—almost midnight

Frustrated, partly because of the cloying heat and partly because Robyn still had not tried to consummate their marriage, Georgine kicked the bedcovers off. Oh, these past several days, he had been attentive as always, even sharing several more of those soul-shattering kisses and a few breath-stealing caresses too.

But the dashed, obstinate man went no further.

And she knew full well Doctor Tinsdale had not forbidden marital relations.

Even now, heat scorched her cheeks upon recalling the disconcerting conversation.

Blushing and stammering, she awkwardly asked the physician during his last visit if her shoulder had healed enough to permit conjugal relations. He agreed it had, as long as she and Robyn took care with what positions they practiced.

Positions?

There are more than one?

Well, that certainly provided more education than she expected or needed from the good doctor.

Mustering up every ounce of courage while firmly stamping her mortification into the ground, she then braved asking Doctor Tinsdale if he had conveyed that sensitive information about her ability to participate in intimacy to Robyn.

After giving her a long, considering glance—and she swore he hid a small smile, but his mustache made it impossible to tell for certain—he finally shook his head.

"No, Mrs. Fitzlloyd. I believe that is a conversation best left to you and your husband."

Bother and blast.

Surely even a green girl could contrive a more subtle enticement than pointing at the blasted mattress.

Georgine had tried to broach the delicate subject with Robyn.

She truly had.

Thrice, as a matter of fact.

Last week, while playing Backgammon, she had leaned forward and whispered, "Sometimes, the surest way to win is to take a risk... and put all one's pieces into play at once."

"Indeed," Robyn said with a triumphant grin as he trounced her thoroughly. Again. "I hope you do not use that strategy when placing wagers for the *Ladies of Opportunity*."

Smug dolt.

A few days later, when strolling in the garden after supper, she eyed the abundant flower beds before saying brightly, "Matilda has such a gift with flowers and plants. Though if the *seeds* had never been planted, we would be standing next to an empty patch, wouldn't we?"

"Tis a wondrous thing, how God orchestrated plants to grow." Robyn plucked a yellow rose and presented it to her. "For you, my love."

Georgine had hidden a frown as she sniffed the delicate, silken petals.

Was he deliberately being thickheaded?

She had said *seeds*, for pity's sake.

Seeds!

Only last evening in the library, Georgine had become positively brazen as a doxie—or at least she thought she had. She pulled a brown leather volume from the shelf and then sighed.

"I cannot abide another dull night." She gave Robyn what she believed was a coy glance and an inviting smile, then added, "I'd rather do something... more entertaining...."

Robyn plucked the book from her fingertips and skimmed the title.

"*The Merchant's and Manufacturer's Commercial Dictionary*." He flipped it open and pointed to a word. "Wefting: Passing the horizontal threads (weft) over and under the vertical threads (warp) in weaving."

"I doubt, sweeting, that you will find this book the least bit entertaining." He chuckled, his shoulders shaking with mirth as he passed the book back to her. "It might put you straight to sleep, however."

She truly wanted to box his ears, and might have done so if she had two good arms.

Oh, the odious, wonderful, obstinate, darling, splendid, contrary, endearing, vexing man.

Sighing, she sat up and swung her legs off the bed.

After swiping her unbound hair from her shoulders, she

stood, her linen shift settling around her calves. The stifling heat made wearing a regular night rail impossible. As it was, she could scarcely sleep, damp with sweat, not to mention her thoughts constantly wandering to Robyn in his chamber.

Did he sleep in the nude?

She waved her hand before her face to cool her scorching cheeks at such a provocative image.

Curving her bare toes into the cool wood floor, she yawned and stretched, taking care not to over-extend her healing arm. After two and a half months, she no longer required a sling, but that didn't mean she could cavort about like an energetic toddler.

With the draperies and windows wide open to allow any hint of a breeze to cool the room, silvery moonlight illuminated her chamber.

She glimpsed herself in the carved mahogany cheval glass.

Pivoting until the mirror reflected her entire form, she stared.

Was there something wrong with her—beyond her healing shoulder?

Is that why Robyn hadn't tried to bed her?

She understood his reticence in the beginning.

After all, they had married under duress, and her shoulder was not healed. Plus, she hadn't exactly been warm and receptive...

In point of fact, she'd behaved like a lamb led to slaughter and had stipulated no relations for six months.

Off-putting, to be sure.

Cocking her head, Georgine took ruthless inventory of her reflection in the glass.

Of average height, her figure tended toward willowiness, yet she was not without feminine substance.

Her eyes were her best feature.

Her attention lit on her shoulder, and she pulled the light fabric of the shift aside, baring her scar.

The jagged two-inch mark had become a pinkish-white pucker.

Ugly, but an improvement from the screaming crimson of weeks ago.

Would Robyn find the scar repugnant?

Squaring her shoulder, she notched her chin upward.

There was only one way to find out.

Before Georgine could talk herself out of her rash decision, she marched to her chamber door, flung it open, and proceeded down the dark corridor.

Robyn's room lay at the end, facing the rear of the house.

She refused to allow herself to speculate on his reaction... or hers if he rejected her.

Chest tight, her heart beating against her ribs like a captured lark in a cage, and her breath coming in shallow rasps, she edged along the carpet, using the wall to guide her in the dim light.

The house breathed with its own quiet life.

A sultry wind drifted through the open windows, stirring the heavy curtains so they whispered against the walls. Each languid gust carried the faintest sigh, a cooling caress against the oppressive heat. From deep within the timbers, the wood answered with muted creaks, as though the beams shifted in their sleep. The floorboards flexed here and there, stretching and settling with a contented sigh.

Halfway there, she almost turned tail and ran back to her bedchamber.

She set her jaw.

You are made of sterner stuff.

If you play the craven now, you shall regret it in the morning.

More than just the morning.

When had she begun to love Robyn so irrevocably?

At what moment had he become essential to her very existence?

Why did his nearness—and the longing for more—command her every thought?

Georgine's love compelled her forward.

She must know, one way or the other.

Once outside Robyn's door, she paused, willing her heart to steady to a normal cadence.

What would she say to him?

As she raised her hand to knock, the door swung open.

Robyn stood there wearing a black and gold striped banyan, tied at the waist, but gaping open, as if he'd thrown it on in a hurry or as an afterthought. No slippers covered his feet, peeking from the robe's hem.

Was he *naked* beneath his robe?

She swallowed, nervous but excited too.

A lamp burned low in the background, the meager light failing to reach the chamber's corners.

Over his broad shoulder, Georgine inspected the purely masculine decor.

Buff walls with polished wood trim framed the chamber. Dominating the room rose a mahogany four-poster, hung with heavy bottle-green damask, shot with gold bed curtains, and spread with a matching coverlet.

Cream pillows softened the display, while the same green-and-gold draperies stirred in the open casement windows. A Turkish carpet in bottle green, crimson, black, and gilt anchored the room.

His bedchamber suited him.

Her attention dropped to the light smattering of silky curls upon Robyn's chest, and she had the most peculiar urge to graze her fingertips through the curly hairs. Her stomach—and lower still—tautened in a foreign, but not unpleasant, fashion.

Instead, she let her hand fall to her side.

Upon seeing her standing at the threshold of his chamber, hair tousled as if he had tossed and turned for hours as she had, his warm brown eyes widened.

"Georgine?"

He raked his hooded, sleep-heavy gaze over her, pausing a half-second too long at the dark shadows her light chemise failed to conceal completely.

"Is something wrong?

"Are you ill?

"Does your shoulder pain you?

"Should I call for the physician?"

His questions came rapidly, one after the other, giving her no opportunity to answer.

"*Shh.*" Laughing, she put two fingers on his mouth, both astounded and exhilarated at her daring.

His lips presented a tantalizing paradox—unexpectedly firm, yet also silken soft.

How Georgine yearned to have those lips upon hers again.

"I am fine, Robyn." Then added when a doubtful pucker wrinkled his forehead. "Truly, I am."

The two creases on his forehead revealed he remained unconvinced. "I cannot imagine a reason you are not abed at this hour unless something is amiss."

In for a penny, in for a pound.

Georgine inhaled, bracing herself. "Nothing amiss that sharing your bed would not remedy."

There.

She had said it.

Asked her husband to bed her.

Well, practically said it.

She wasn't so audacious or bold as to demand he take her to his bed and rid her of her virginity.

Yet if subtlety failed—*again*—Georgine supposed she could topple onto the mattress, tug her shift scandalously high, and hope he took the hint.

Robyn's eyes went impossibly round, and if the moment hadn't been so fraught with tension, and her nerves were not dancing about like drunken sailors, she might have laughed at his flabbergasted expression.

A moment later, smoldering fire lit his eyes, and he regarded her with half-closed lids, a primal smile of delight splitting his face. "Forgive my blunt speech, but I want to make certain I understand, sweetheart. You wish to come to bed with me?"

"Oh, for pity's sake, Robyn.

"How forward must I be?

"I've hinted for days."

She threw her hands up in frustration, her shoulder twinging the merest bit at the sudden movement. "At this rate, I half-fear I shall expire of old age before you think to tumble me properly."

Laughing heartily, Robyn threw his head back, his Adam's apple standing out against the strong column of his throat.

Chagrined, she stiffened. "It is not *that* funny."

Embarrassment made her voice sharper than she had intended.

"Come here, darling."

Robyn pulled her against his chest.

As always, he smelled superb, and there was something deliciously wicked about rubbing her cheek against his chest hair.

Why had no one ever mentioned how tantalizing and seductive a man's chest could be?

"Don't take offense, sweet." His voice had become a throaty purr, and a shiver of awareness sluiced through her. "I assure you, I'm more than delighted at your forwardness."

Georgine angled her head upward, expecting to meet his humor-filled gaze. However, her stomach plummeted to her feet when she recognized desire, raging and barely constrained, simmering in his irises instead of jollity. "You don't mind?"

"*Mind*?" Firming his embrace, Robyn spoke into her hair. "Good God, no. I've marched down that corridor dozens of times these past days, only to turn around for fear you would not receive me."

Georgine could not prevent her jubilant smile before admitting shyly, "I've been waiting for you, hoping you would come. Doctor Tinsdale assured me my shoulder does not prevent intimacy as long as we are mindful of certain positions."

"He did, did he?" Distinct irony weighted Robyn's husky tenor.

"I don't know what he means by positions." She crinkled her nose.

Robyn chuckled again. "I do."

His tender expression grew serious as he searched her face. "Are you certain, Georgine?"

"Absolutely." Placing her palm against his bristly jaw, she nodded. "I love you, Robyn."

"Thank God." He closed his eyes, his thick lashes a dark fringe on his high cheekbones. When he opened his eyes, she gasped at the adoration shining there. Touching his forehead to hers, he whispered hoarsely. "I've loved you for so long and didn't dare hope you could ever come to love me too."

Tears blurred her vision. "I truly do. I'm sorry it took me so long to realize it, but I want to be your wife in every way."

"I would carry you across the threshold, but I fear I'd injure your shoulder." Keeping one arm wrapped around her waist, he guided her into his bedchamber and shut the door with his other hand.

As they approached his massive bed, she glanced upward. "Robyn?"

"Aye?"

"What, exactly, did Doctor Tinsdale mean by 'different positions?'"

Robyn untied the ribbons on one shoulder of her chemise, then bent to kiss her bare skin.

She gasped and clutched his banyan.

Lord, have mercy.

"Why don't I show you, my love?"

EPILOGUE

Fernleigh House Gardens

A fortnight later—late afternoon

Nodding at his cousin, Shelby Tellinger, Robyn strolled among their guests as he made his way to the head table beneath the marquee. After two weeks of whirlwind preparations, the day of the promised wedding reception had arrived.

Wearing a shimmering pink and silver gown, with diamonds at her throat, ears, and wrist, Georgine had never been more beautiful.

Robyn curved his mouth in a self-deprecating grin.

He thought that of her every day.

But it was true.

She grew more lovely and precious to him every day in every way.

Though the reason for her forced recuperation at his house might have been reprehensible, he couldn't regret the circumstances, for the calamity had resulted in happiness he had never dreamed possible.

His heart full of joy, he glanced around again.

A few more than a hundred guests had joined him and Georgine for the belated wedding reception and milled about the manicured gardens sipping champagne, lemonade, or punch.

Hetty Twigg chatted with Matilda and a couple of other ladies. She'd already secured another position—this time as a traveling companion to two spinster sisters. Thanks to her insightful wager, she now possessed a handsome sum and would never be at an employer's mercy again.

Bully for her.

Reluctant to press charges, Reverend Goodfellow had urged Mrs. Wynecott to retire to Dorchester, far from London and the censure she deserved for her thievery.

In Robyn's opinion, she suffered too little consequence for her actions, but the reverend insisted on forgiveness and compassion.

If the woman possessed an ounce of wisdom, she would shut her mouth and live out the remainder of her life in obscurity.

In truth, that was as likely as Prinny squeezing into last year's pantaloons.

The Earl of Wainthorpe raised a hand in greeting, and Robyn returned the gesture.

From across the lawn, the Earl of Renshaw nodded, as did Viscount Sethwick.

The aristocrats who had come to his and Georgine's defense at Gunter's Tea Shop had kept their promise to attend the reception. The married chaps had brought their lady wives.

Robyn would be bound, some peeresses had met Georgine

before, although they were careful to keep their expressions polite and friendly when he'd introduced them.

It wasn't entirely impossible that some of those ladies had ventured a wager with the *Ladies of Opportunity*, but Hades would trumpet Handel's *Hallelujah Chorus* before Georgine revealed a single patron's name.

Her friends remained equally closed-mouthed.

Robyn admired their integrity.

"Happy, darling?" He nuzzled Georgine's ear, uncaring that it was not the thing to show affection in public.

Waving her fan, she gave him a siren's glance. "You know I am, naughty man. I showed you how much only two hours ago."

And by all that was holy, Robyn would never regard the library the same.

No, indeed.

An imbecilic grin split his face.

Robyn didn't give a rap.

He signaled to Bichard, who dutifully rang the gong, indicating the guests should make their way to the supper tables. No longer restricted to an invalid's diet, Georgine and Mrs. Fennick spent hours planning the menu.

As everyone took their seats, he remained standing behind his chair.

If a man were fortunate, he married only once.

If he were blessed, he would wed for love.

Somehow, Fate has smiled upon him, bestowing both.

He skimmed his gaze over the crowd, smiling at his friends and family, who were there to celebrate with him and his bride.

Claire Granlund sank into a chair beside Aubriella Matherfield, and Quinten Honeybrook promptly sat on Mrs.

Granlund's other side. She slid him an annoyed sideways glance before directing her focus across the table.

What the blazed went on with those two?

Georgine slipped her hand into his.

"How is your shoulder, darling?" He still worried she would over-exert herself.

"Stiff, but not sore." She grinned up at him. "But then you don't allow me to carry anything heavier than a feather. The doctor says I need to work on strengthening my arm and shoulder."

She chuckled, the sound a husky tinkle. "When I told you about my father's abusive behavior, Robyn, I did not mean for you to coddle me like an infant."

"I know, my love." He pressed the palm of his hand into the small of her back. "Forgive me."

"Always, darling." She leaned into his side, adoration etched upon her features.

For him.

The wonder of that rare gift would boggle his mind for the rest of his life.

Once everyone had taken their seats, Robyn raised his wineglass and cleared his throat. "Ladies and gentlemen."

Turning their attention toward Robyn and Georgine, everyone stood, glasses in hand.

He took Georgine's hand.

"Pray, raise your glasses with me. To my bride, whose grace and constancy outshine every jewel in Christendom. May our days be blessed with harmony, and our hearts ever beat as one. To my beloved wife."

"To the bride," echoed around the tables.

After everyone took a sip, several guests murmured approbations.

"Hear, hear."

"Just so."

The gentlemen bowed toward Georgine, and the ladies smiled and nodded.

Her eyes shining, Georgine raised her glass. "To us."

"To us, my love."

But instead of taking a drink of champagne, Robyn brushed his mouth across hers.

"Forever and always."

THE END

I hope you enjoyed BETTER NOT BET A BLUESTOCKING and watching Robyn and Georgine's romantic tale unfold. If you'd like to leave a review, please visit your online bookstore of choice. I would be so grateful.

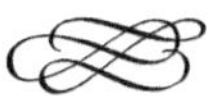

**Rochester, England
9 December 1817
Early afternoon**

"Miss Winterborne?"

Mrs. Sabella Thackpenny's sleep-thickened, warbly voice yanked Joy from her pleasant daydream about where she'd spend her half-day off this Saturday.

Walking in The Vines Gardens?

Browsing the shelves at Barclay's Book Shoppe and Emporium?

Or—the thought nearly made her sigh aloud in anticipation—perhaps enjoying a cup of *strong,* sweet tea with milk at that quaint tea shop on High Street where she and her friend Mercy Feathers had enjoyed maid of honor tarts two years ago?

Mercy was the governess for two young charges here in Rochester.

Had it truly been two years since Joy had seen her friend?

Lips pressed tight, she shook her head the slightest bit.

It didn't seem possible that much time had passed.

She clearly remembered the Christmas decorations and gingerbread cookies that day. She could still almost smell the evergreens and the cinnamon, cloves, and ginger. Aromas she'd not enjoyed the pleasure of since.

Joy missed the other young women from Haven House and Academy for the Enrichment of Young Women who had become her sisters in every way except for by blood. She especially missed Mercy, Chasity Nobel, and Purity Mayfield. The four of them had shared a room at the academy for as long as Joy could remember.

All of the cast-off girls who'd ever called Haven House and Academy for the Enrichment of Young Women their home had shared a middle name too. Shepard. The name was a slightly altered version of the kindly but strict and extremely pious Hester Shepherd's own surname.

That sweet, Godly woman had bestowed a Biblical given name upon each discarded child in her loving care. Mrs. Shepherd, now a spinster in her sixth decade, vowed she adored the girls she'd raised since infancy like her own daughters.

The honorary *missus* before her last name was a matter of formality. No proper instructor was ever addressed as a *miss*.

As Mrs. Shepherd had been taking in unwanted charges— all by-blows in one form or another of the wealthy or aristocracy—for two-and-one-half decades, she'd been a mother to nearly seventy girls. All of which she'd raised to be prayerful, moral young women despite their unfortunate beginnings.

"Each of you are a gift from our Lord. He has a purpose in everything. 'All things work together for good to those who love God,'" Mrs. Shepherd quoted to her girls from the scriptures. "Even your presence at Haven House and Academy for the Enrichment of Young Women is no accident. Never forget it, my dears," she admonished fondly.

What was more, Mrs. Shepherd and her discreet staff had provided every girl with an education and skills for respectable employment. Not, however, entirely out of benevolence. Haven House and Academy for the Enrichment of Young Women and Mrs. Shepherd had been well-compensated for her discretion and the girls' decorous upbringing.

Joy was eternally grateful. She missed the headmistress's light-hearted scolds and contagious laughter. Naturally, they corresponded—quite regularly as a matter of fact. But a piece of paper slashed with tiny, neat script was no substitute for one of Mrs. Shepherd's soft, comforting rose and violet scented hugs.

How very different was the plump, genial headmistress compared to the pinch-faced woman across the room blinking sleepily behind her spectacles, her mouth pursed in a perpetual grimace of disapproval.

Or perhaps Mrs. Thackpenny's turned down mouth was a result of her recent propensity to pass gas with the offensive regularity and unfortunate exuberance of a barnyard animal. A *large* barnyard animal.

Joy held her breath, hoping her employer would settle back into her nap, which was her habit in the afternoon. She longed to return to her daydream about delicious tea and sweet cakes in a cozy teashop. If she couldn't actually consume the treats, at least Joy could fantasize about doing so.

A slight nasally snore resonated from the afghan covered lump, and tension eased from Joy's spine and shoulders. A few more minutes of peace was a treasured blessing.

Mrs. Thackpenny—*pinchpenny is more apt*—only permitted Joy used tea leaves. Leaves which the difficult widow had already used twice herself. The resulting brew was slightly bronze-tinted water, which scarcely tasted of tea at all.

And no sugar or milk. Ever.

"A body can never economize too much, Miss Winterborne," the rail-thin woman had intoned when she'd first retained Joy as her lady's companion. "You'll learn soon enough that though I'm extremely frugal, I'm not miserly."

Only tightfisted and parsimonious.

"Save a penny, save a pound." As was her wont, Mrs. Thackpenny emphasized the latter colloquialism with a resounding thump of her worse-for-wear cane.

Wasn't the phrase, A penny saved is a penny earned, anyway? Or was it, Look after pennies, and the pounds will look after themselves?

It didn't matter. What did, however, was Mrs. Thackpenny's tightfistedness.

Persuading the woman to part with funds was as difficult as convincing a nun to toss up her habit for a dockside tumble with a salty sea dog—in broad daylight.

Every single month since her arrival, Joy had been obliged to ask for her allowance and carefully count each coin. For her penny-pinching employer had tried to cheat her out of a shilling or two several times.

Honestly, there wasn't any need for her excessive thrift either.

Mrs. Thackpenny's husband, a successful banker, had left her a considerable fortune. Yet the decades-old worn and quite threadbare carpets, draperies, and outdated furnishings remained as a tribute to the long-dead Mr. Ephraim Thackpenny.

The widow owned precisely seven gowns—one for each day of the week. Every one entirely black from collar to hem and as plain as unused paper, without so much as a shiny button to break the bleak monotony.

Head canted, Joy listened for her employer's drowsy murmurings, and when no more sounds came from the woman, decided Mrs. Thackpenny had, indeed, been mumbling in her sleep. A common enough occurrence, in truth.

Joy happily turned her musings toward her half-day off once more.

Mayhap, she'd indulge in all three activities this Saturday.

The merest rebellious smile bent her mouth

Yes, that was precisely what she'd do.

Visit The Vines, the bookstore, *and* the tea shop.

Pure heaven.

A small frown pulled her eyebrows together as she inserted the needle into the fine linen fabric, another handkerchief for her mistress—Mrs. Thackpenny's one indulgence besides her pampered pets.

That was her plan *if* Mrs. Thackpenny actually permitted Joy the half-day she'd been assured of each week when hired by the difficult woman four years ago—no five years next week. There'd also been promises of exciting trips to Bath, the Continent, routs, musicals, soirees, the theater...museums.

None of which had ever manifested. If Joy managed a single, short walk outdoors every week, she counted herself most fortunate.

An unintended sigh slipped past her lips.

All fabrications to entice a young girl with stars in her eyes and dreams of a different, more exciting life clouding her common sense.

Little had Joy known that she was the latest in a long queue of lady's maids retained and dismissed since Mrs. Sabella

Thackpenny had taken a fall a decade before. Hence the need for her cane, and upon the advice of her then physician, Doctor Daggat, she'd conceded the need for a live-in companion.

Companion was a generous term for what Joy was to the woman. She was expected to be on hand for whatever the difficult widow demanded every hour of every day and night.

In truth, Mrs. Thackpenny seldom allowed Joy her half-day and never compensated for the deliberate oversight.

How Joy craved a few hours of desperately needed reprieve from the demanding, cantankerous, never satisfied woman's presence. There was never a word of thanks or appreciation. Just scolds, complaints, reprimands, and the occasional threat of dismissal.

And dash it to ribbons, that was what Joy could look forward to until Mrs. Thackpenny departed this earth, unless she was somehow able to procure another position. With considerable effort, Joy quashed the wave of frustration billowing up from her middle that her errant, uncharitable thoughts brought on.

She closed her eyes and sent up a silent prayer.

Lord, give me the strength and patience I need. Keep me from complaining and help me be grateful. My life could be so much worse.

Her eyes drifted open.

It could be better too.

But, *this* was her lot in life, and she ought to be appreciative. In truth and much to her astonishment, despite her employer's contentious nature, Joy had grown fond of the impossible woman.

At least she held a position, albeit one that paid poorly and consumed all of her waking hours. But a roof over one's head and food in one's belly, even if the fare was bland and unappetizing, accounted for much. That was more than most young women born on the wrong side of the blanket could say or even hope for.

Of course, Mrs. Thackpenny didn't know that particular scandalous detail about Joy's paternity.

Nor would she ever. The very notion made her ill.

A shiver skittered the length of her spine.

For God help her, Joy's position and reputation depended upon that scandal remaining a secret. As did Haven House and Academy for the Enrichment of Young Women's, and the many girls who had ever called the place home.

Mrs. Shepherd made absolutely certain her *girls'* unsavory origins were diligently guarded and hidden. She created respectable faux backgrounds and prepared them for various positions appropriate for gently-bred young ladies.

She was paid handsomely—*very* handsomely—for her exclusive, confidential services too. Surely she'd amassed enough savings to retire in comfort, yet Mrs. Shepherd cheerfully continued in her position.

It struck Joy as peculiar that a parent who was so eager to hide their by-blow or bastard daughter would pay Mrs. Shepherd's exorbitant fee and ensure their illegitimate offspring had a decent future. But then again, there was no understanding the peculiarities of the wealthy or the peerage, in Joy's limited experience.

Odder still were the surnames Mrs. Shepherd dubbed each of her charges with. She vowed the name contained a hint about each girl's familial heritage. Nonetheless, to Joy's knowledge, thus far, not a single former ward had identified either parent.

What difference would it make anyway?

"Miss Winterborne?"

Mrs. Thackpenny's voice pitched higher, and the unfortunate wooden floor—already scarred and scraped—received a pair of undeserved petulant thwacks from her ever-present cane.

Thump. Thump.

"*Where* is my darling Sir Galahad Whiskerton?"

Thump. Thump.

"Miss Win-ter-borne? Are you there?"

Her shrill voice pierced the air once more.

Joy winced as she accidentally pricked her finger.

As if she couldn't hear her crotchety employer's strident tones from the chair less than ten feet away. Rather astonishing that a woman so shrunken and petite could produce such remarkable volume with her reedy voice.

"Yes, Mrs. Thackpenny. Permit me to finish this French knot, please."

Accustomed to her employer's ill-temper, Joy calmly finished her embroidery stitch despite her cold fingers' stiffness.

From beneath her lashes, she cast a yearning glance toward the few insufficient glowing coals in the grate, in front of which Mrs. Thackpenny's small settee was positioned to absorb the stingy warmth the pathetic fire provided.

Was it a sin to covet a smidgen of the sparse warmth for herself?

Little heat radiated past the settee, leaving the rest of the room so frigid, Joy could see her own puffs of breath. She deliberately blew out several, watching the vapor disappear, just to prove her point. Besides the kitchen, this was the warmest room in the house, which wasn't saying much.

The temperature indoors accounted for the two pairs of stockings she wore as well as the housecoat and hand-knitted woolen shawl wrapped around her shoulders and pinned neatly at her bosom with a simple, but elegant silver cross brooch—a parting gift from Mrs. Shepherd. Joy wore fingerless gloves, also hand-knitted, but that didn't prevent the digits from becoming distressingly cold.

As always, because Mrs. Thackpenny preferred a tomb-like atmosphere, the faded burgundy brocade draperies remained closed against the day's chill. Truth be told, Joy would've welcomed meager sunlight streaming through the floor to ceiling arched windows. She couldn't help but think Mrs. Thackpenny would also benefit from a spot of sun.

It couldn't be good for a soul to be shut up indoors with no light or fresh air for weeks on end. God only knew Joy felt the effects of such confinement. Humans weren't meant to huddle in the dark like frightened insects or creep about in the gloom like earthworms or moles.

"You know I cannot bear for Whiskers to be away from me," the elderly woman complained in a child's sulky voice—a strident voice which grated along Joy's spine like sharp talons scraping the bones.

She's old and lonely, Joy reminded herself. Be charitable.

Her husband died when she was not much older than you.

She has no children or remaining family and few friends.

In an attempt to harness her vexation, Joy recited one of the many scriptures Mrs. Shepherd had drilled into her and the other girls.

A kind word turns away wrath.

Kindness had never worked with Mrs. Thackpenny before.

Determined to harness her unkind thoughts, Joy repeated the verse twice more.

A kind word turns away wrath.

A kind word turns away wrath.

Screwing her face into a grimace, she released a noiseless snort.

Pshaw.

Such exercises were useless. Joy would never completely master her thoughts when it came to Mrs. Thackpenny.

The widow could vex the most pious of priests, and Joy had never claimed the benevolence or compassion of a man of the cloth. Nevertheless, with a determined set of her chin and after a deep breath to regain her equanimity, Joy said, "Indeed, I do understand how precious Sir Whiskerton and Poppet are to you."

And she truly did. For, the truth of it was, Joy was also lonely.

Unbearably so at times.

She missed the other girls' companionship at Haven House and Academy for the Enrichment of Young Women. There'd been no opportunity to make new friends since she'd taken her current position.

Except for Mercy Feathers, she hadn't seen any of her former friends either. Joy did correspond with several. Only sporadically, however, since foolscap, ink, and postage were luxuries she could ill afford, and Mrs. Thackpenny only grudgingly shared the former.

Joy's isolation was especially trying this time of year when evidence of the upcoming Yuletide was everywhere. Why, just yesterday, a gleaming claret-colored coach had trundled by with a festive evergreen, holly, and gold beribboned wreath secured to the back.

Now that person possessed the holiday spirit.

Mrs. Thackpenny didn't observe Christmas-tide with so much as a sprig of mistletoe or a cinnamon bun. Holly and gingerbread were taboo to the crusty widow. On the other hand, Mrs. Shepherd had literally decked the halls, doorways, and mantels of Haven House and Academy for the Enrichment of Young Women.

Such delicious, mouth-watering smells had filled the corridors for days in advance of the holiday. Beaming, she'd present each girl a gift Christmas morning. A festive time was had by all, playing parlor games, singing around the pianoforte, skating on the lake–if the weather cooperated–and of course, eating scrumptious holiday foods.

Joy particularly favored mulled cider and Christmas pudding.

More than once, Joy wondered what her life would have been like if she'd waited for another position to become available. If she hadn't naively believed the false promises Mrs. Thackpenny had made to a young, impressionable girl.

Staring blankly at the heavily draped windows, she lifted a shoulder.

Would I be better off than this life of drudgery?

I hope you enjoyed this free preview of
A LADY'S SCANDALOUS KISS
Secrets of Scandalous Ladies
Book One

If you'd like to keep reading, please scan the QR code.

Thank you for reading BETTER NOT BET A BLUESTOCKING.

Georgine's recovery at the Fitzlloyds was not precisely improper. She was a close friend of Matilda's, and at twenty-six, she no longer required a chaperone. However, for those determined to see scandal where none existed, the arrangement could have provoked unpleasant whispers.

St. Winifred's Church is entirely fictional. While I could have chosen a real church on the outskirts of London, none existed near the imagined location of Fernleigh House, so I created one to suit the story. While it is possible Reverend Goodfellow could have had Mrs. Wynecott brought up on charges, I decided, as a man of God, he should act charitably instead.

In 1819, medical treatment for gunshot wounds was primitive by modern standards. Recovery, if the patient survived the high risk of infection, often took months—especially if bone was damaged, as in Georgine's case.

Although sanitization was not widely practiced, I made Doctor Tinsdale something of a pioneer in that regard. The lack of proper treatment and physical therapy would likely have left Georgine with significant limitations in her arm's mobility. However, as this is fiction, I allowed her to escape with only a little stiffness and a slight restriction in range of motion.

Although a joint first edition of *Northanger Abbey and Persuasion* was published in 1818, only 1750 copies were created. Matilda's copy would have been a rare edition indeed.

I have mentioned Gunter's Tea Shop in other books, but this time, I wanted Regina to request a new flavor of ice. In 1819, the latest additions to the menu were pistachio, white coffee, and brown bread. Savory ices were as popular as sweet treats, but I could not picture a young girl pleading for white coffee or brown bread ice.

One other quick note about delicacies served at Gunter's. Water ice was a frozen confection of fruit juice, sugar, and water, churned smooth like a sorbet—not ice water.

I referred to a few peers in the Gunter's Tea Shop scene. Each of those nobles has their own story, which you can read about in their books.

Maxwell, Duke of Pennington, WHAT WOULD A DUKE DO?, Dukes Come Calling series

Lucan, Duke of Harcourt, HEARTBREAK AND HONOR, Highland Heather Romancing a Scot: Castle Brides Series

Ewan, Viscount Sethwick, THE HIGHLANDER'S HEIRESS, Highland Heather Romancing a Scot: Castle Brides Series

Pierce, Earl of Wainthorpe, EARL OF WAINTHORPE, For the Love of an Earl Series

Sanford, Earl of Renshaw, EARL OF RENSHAW, For the Love of an Earl Series.

Whether you are discovering my books for the first time or

have been a devoted fan for years, I truly hope you found a delightful escape with Robyn and Georgine!

For discounted series bundles and other specials, visit my bookstore: collettecameronbooks.com

With heartfelt thanks and happy reading,

Until next time,

Hugs,

Collette Cameron

If you haven't joined Collette's exclusive mailing list click on QR image to sign up! You'll get access to exclusive content, sneak peeks, contests, giveaways, and more...

(P.S. No spam!)

https://collettecameronbooks.com/freegift

Collette loves to hear from readers.
You can contact her via her website: collettecameronbooks.com.
Or email her directly at collette@collettecameronbooks.com.

You can also follow Collette on social media:
Facebook: https://www.facebook.com/ColletteCameronNovels/
Instagram: https://instagram.com/collettecameronauthor/
Goodreads: https://www.goodreads.com/collettecameron
Book Bub: https://www.bookbub.com/authors/collettecameron

Pinterest: http://www.pinterest.com/colletteauthor/
YouTube: https://www.youtube.com/@ColletteCameronAuthor

Giggles are Guaranteed
Collette's Cheris Reader Group

https://www.facebook.com/groups/CollettesCheris/

If you love to chat about all things romance-book related and enjoy taking part in fun and engaging live events, contests, and giveaways join **Collette's Chèris VIP Reader Group, https://www.facebook.com/groups/CollettesCheris/,** my exclusive private book group on Facebook.

Giggles are guaranteed!

Hope to see you there,
Collette Cameron®

ABOUT THE AUTHOR

COLLETTE CAMERON®

USA Today Bestselling author Collette Cameron® is renowned for her captivating, humorous, and heartwarming Scottish and Regency historical romance novels. With over 65 published titles, over 1.6 million books sold around the world, and multiple writing awards to her credit, Collette is a well-known author in the world of historical romance.

Readers love her witty and relatable characters including daring rogues, dashing scoundrels, and the strong and spirited heroines who capture their hearts. From the rugged highlands to the refined drawing rooms of Regency England, Collette's novels will transport you to another time and place, where love and adventure are just a page away.

Collette's Sweet-to-Spicy Timeless Romances® are the perfect escape for readers looking for romantic escape, poignant inspiration, engaging humor, and entertaining stories.

Based in the Pacific Northwest, Collette is surrounded by the lush greenery and rainy skies that inspire her writing. She dreams of one day splitting her time between the Pacific Northwest and Scotland. In the meantime, she indulges in her love of all things cobalt blue, dachshunds, chocolate, and of course, crafting her next historical romance.

Blue Rose Romance® LLC
collette@collettecameronbooks.com
collettecameronbooks.com

~

FOR THE LOVE OF AN EARL (Wicked Earls' Club)

A Humorous Aristocrat and Wallflower

Regency Romance Adventure

~

HEART OF A SCOT

A Passionate Enemies to Lovers

Scottish Highlander Historical Mystery

Romance Adventure

To Love a Highland Laird — Book 1

To Redeem a Highland Rogue — Book 2

To Seduce a Highland Scoundrel — Book 3

To Woo a Highland Warrior — Book 4

To Enchant a Highland Earl — Book 5

To Defy a Highland Duke — Book 6

To Marry a Highland Marauder — Book 7

To Bargain with a Highland Buccaneer — Book 8

A Christmas Kiss for the Highlander — Book 9

～

HIGHLAND HEATHER ROMANCING A SCOT: CASTLE BRIDES

A Passionate Enemies to Lovers Second Chance

Scottish Highlander Mystery Romance

Heart of a Highlander — Prequel

The Viscount's Vow — Book 1

The Highlander's Heiress — Book 2

The Earl's Enticement — Book 3

Triumph and Treasure — Book 4

Virtue and Valor — Book 5

Heartbreak and Honor — Book

Scandal's Splendor — Book 7

Passion and Plunder — Book 8

Wishes and Wonder — Book 9

A Yuletide Highlander — Book 10

~

LADIES OF OPPORTUNITY
A Bluestockings and Rogues Opposites Attract
Regency Mystery Christmas Romance

The Wallflower's Wild Wager — Book 1
The Spinster's Secret Stake, Book 2
Better Not Bet a Bluestocking – Book 3

~

SECRETS OF SCANDALOUS LADIES
A Romantic Class Difference Forced Proximity
Regency Romance with Aristocrats

A Lady's Scandalous Kiss — Book 1
No Lady for the Lord — Book 2
Love Lessons for a Lady — Book 3
His One and Only Lady — Book 4
Never a Proper Lady — Book 5
Lady Tempts a Rogue — Book 6

~

THE CULPEPPER MISSES
A Humorous Wallflower Family Saga
Regency Romantic Comedy

The Earl and the Spinster — Book 1
The Marquis and the Vixen — Book 2

THE HONORABLE ROGUES®
A Second Chance Redeemable Rogue
and Wallflower Regency Romance

9 781966 608753 3